The Eagles' Child

The
Eagles' Child

Barbara Ford

Macmillan Publishing Company New York

Collier Macmillan Canada Toronto

Maxwell Macmillan International Publishing Group

New York Oxford Singapore Sydney

Macmillan Publishing Company
866 Third Avenue, New York, NY 10022
Collier Macmillan Canada, Inc.
1200 Eglinton Avenue East, Suite 200
Don Mills, Ontario M3C 3N1
First Edition   Printed in the United States of America

10   9   8   7   6   5   4   3   2   1

The text of this book is set in 12 point Janson.

Library of Congress Cataloging-in-Publication Data
Ford, Barbara.
The eagles' child / by Barbara Ford.—1st ed.   p.   cm.
Summary: Spending the summer in New York City with her
godmother while her mother is in Africa, Amy has many adjustments
to make, especially when her divorced father gets
romantically involved with her godmother.
ISBN 0-02-735405-9
[1. New York (N.Y.)—Fiction.   2. Parent and child—Fiction.]   I. Title.
PZ7.F752345Eag   1990   [Fic]—dc20   90-5633   CIP   AC

For my writers group,
which spent almost as much time
as I did with Amy

The Eagles' Child

Chapter One

W e had the burgers at the kitchen table, where we always eat when there isn't any company. Mine was burned around the edges, the way I like it.

"Guess I won't get any burgers in Africa," said my mother.

"What do they eat there?"

"*I* don't know. Chickens, probably. And goat meat." My mother giggled. "That's what they tell me, anyway. Aren't you glad you're not going?"

I was. And I wasn't. Everyone said the place in Africa where my mother was going was too hot and wet and buggy for me. Besides, there wouldn't be anything for me to do while my mother was collecting folktales. So I had to stay with my horrible cousin Jessica while my mother was away. Practically anything would be better than Jessica.

"I have to go to New York to pick up my visa tomorrow," said my mother. "Why don't you come with me? Maybe we can have lunch with Liz."

"Okay." Liz is my godmother. She was my mother's roommate in college.

The reason my mother was going to Africa was that she won this fellowship, which is a kind of prize. They let her go anywhere in the world for the summer to do her work, so she was going to Africa to collect folktales. My mother teaches folklore at the university. She's very smart.

"That's what I like about paper plates," said my mother. She stuffed the greasy plates into the wastebasket under the sink. "Let's go to the ice cream shop for dessert."

We were eating Double Fudge Wundafuls in the car when we saw Brad. Brad is the one who's in love with my mother now. Someone is always in love with her, because she's so beautiful.

"Kathy!" Brad smiled at my mother as he walked toward us. He leaned his arm on the car door.

"Kathy!" he said again, just like he hadn't seen my mother the day before.

"Hi, Brad." My mother took a big spoonful of her Double Fudge Wundaful. Double Fudge Wundafuls have all this special stiff chocolate that's like glue. I love Double Fudge Wundafuls.

"I can't believe you'll be leaving soon. Three months!" Brad shook his head. "Let's have lunch tomorrow."

"I'll be in the city tomorrow afternoon. Besides, we're going to the concert tomorrow night."

Brad didn't look at me. He never looks at me. "Why don't I come over tonight?" he asked. "There's a good program on the scaly anteater on public television."

"Too tired," said my mother, starting the engine. She handed Brad the plastic cups our Wundafuls came in. "Drop these in the can, will you, Brad? See you tomorrow."

We drove out of the parking lot. I looked back. Brad was just standing there, staring after the car. I don't like Brad—he never talks to me. I hope my mother doesn't get married to him. He asks her to marry him almost every week, she says.

"It's too bad Brad is so boring," said my mother. "But what a body!"

"I don't like him."

"He has tenure, you know."

I knew. Tenure means when you work for a

3

university, you can't get fired. My mother doesn't have tenure.

When we got home, I fed Pink, my white rat. Pink is pure, pure white except for his pink nose and feet and the inside of his ears. He's beautiful.

In the living room, my mother was lying on the couch, watching TV. I moved a pile of books from the chair to the table so I could sit down.

Crash!

All the books were on the floor, along with a coffee cup and a saucer and a plant Brad gave my mother.

"I never liked that plant," said my mother. "Let's clean it up tomorrow."

My mother doesn't like to clean. Neither do I.

The next day we took the train to New York. I like the train. You can see in people's back windows.

"Do you mind staying with my sister and Jessica while I'm gone?" asked my mother.

"No."

"You're lying." My mother smoothed my hair and smiled at me. My hair is brown. Hers is blond.

"Jessica is awful right now, I know," said my mother. "If only your father could take you. But it's impossible."

I looked out the window. In the backyard of a house, two boys were playing catch.

I'd have liked to stay with my father, but he

didn't have any room. He used to be in advertising, but he gave it up to be an artist. He has this little apartment in New York, in a big building where only artists live. When I go to my father's, we have to eat on the floor because the table is full of paints, and I have to sleep in a sleeping bag.

"I don't know why Carl has to paint such big paintings," said my mother. "You can hardly fit a cockroach into that place."

The train went by someone's back porch. There were people sitting on the porch, drinking something.

"It's not that he's selling them," my mother went on. "He hardly sells enough to pay the rent for that miserable place. And of course there's no money for you!"

I didn't look at my mother. I knew her face would be all angry looking, the way it always is when she talks about my father. I wished my father sold his paintings. I wished he had a bigger apartment. I wished I could see him every week, instead of just one weekend a month, like the custody agreement says.

"That's why I have to go to Africa. You know that, don't you? It will help me get tenure. If I get tenure, we can buy a house. We can have some *security.*"

"Can I have a big-screen TV like Jessica's if you get tenure?"

"Why not?" My mother put her arm around my shoulder and hugged me.

I put my head back against the seat. After a while, the places the train went through weren't so nice anymore. The houses were dark and close together, and there weren't any yards. My mother didn't look out the window. She was reading some folktales in a book.

"Tell me a folktale," I said. My mother used to tell me all these folktales when I was little, and she still tells them to me when I ask her.

She told me a tale about a leopard that planted a garden and ate all the animals that came there to eat until he met this very smart rabbit. It was a good folktale.

After we got my mother's visa, we went to the restaurant where we were going to meet Liz. The restaurant was in the basement of an awful-looking old building. A sign on the window said:

LA PETITE MAISON

"This is a French restaurant," I said.

"That's right," said my mother as we went down the steps.

"I don't like French food. It looks funny. And it's all covered with guck."

"Liz!" My mother was waving at Liz, who was sitting at a table in the corner. It was so dark I could hardly see her.

6

"Kathy! Amy!"

Liz is a writer. She writes books for young adults, which means teenagers like Jessica. My mother and Liz talked while I looked at the menu. It was in French and English but I could only understand the English. It sounded awful: "Braised Breast of Capon bathed in a delicate white wine sauce." Yuck!

"Can I have a hamburger?" I asked. "And fries?"

"A . . . burger?" asked Liz.

"No," said my mother.

Liz said the closest thing to a hamburger was Boeuf à la Mode, so I ordered that. It was a piece of beef with all this gloppy yellow stuff on it. I scraped off as much as I could.

Liz isn't beautiful like my mother, but she looks nice. She's tall and has lots of dark, curly hair. She smiles a lot and waves her hands. She was excited because one of her books had been nominated for an award.

"It's an honor just to be nominated," said Liz.

"Here's to awards," said my mother, raising her wine glass.

"And tenure," said Liz.

They giggled and clinked their glasses together.

"You know, it's funny," said Liz. "I mean, my writing for children when I don't have any children. Why, I hardly ever see any children. I should get in contact with young people. Spend time with them. Yes, I'll have to do that someday, when I have time."

She took a big gulp of wine.

My mother looked at me. I looked at her. I could stay with Liz in the city, I thought! Then I could see my father every week! And I wouldn't have to be with my horrible cousin Jessica. I smiled at my mother and nodded my head a little tiny bit. I knew she knew what I meant.

My mother smiled back and then she looked at Liz. "Liz, I have an idea. You want more contact with young people. Amy needs a place to stay for the three months I'm gone. She was going to stay with my sister, but my sister's daughter is difficult. She and Amy hate each other." My mother looked at me out of the corner of her eyes. "Why doesn't Amy stay with you?"

Liz swallowed too much wine and coughed. Her face got all red. "Kathy, I only have a one-bedroom apartment!" she said when she stopped coughing. "And I work at home."

"A big one-bedroom apartment," said my mother. "And it's only for three months."

"But, Kathy," said Liz in this little tiny voice, "I've always lived alone. I'm used to . . . my privacy."

"Let's go to the ladies' room," said my mother to Liz. They both got up.

"Amy, while we're gone, why don't you order

Sorbet à la Maison for all of us," said Liz. "It's like ice cream."

While they were gone, the waiter walked right by our table without stopping.

"We want some dessert," I said in a loud voice. A man at the next table turned around and smiled at me.

The waiter stopped. He was very old and not much taller than me when I stand up. He said something like "Mamzelldayzeer?"

"Is Sorbet à la Maison really like ice cream?" I asked.

"Eees very good, sorbet," said the waiter.

I could see that I couldn't really talk to him. "Okay, three," I said.

By the time the three Sorbets à la Maison came, my mother and Liz were back. The sorbet was this weird shade of green. I took a spoonful. It didn't taste like ice cream at all. Nothing there tasted like real food.

"It's lettuce sorbet," said Liz. "They're into healthful French food here, you know." Then she looked at me. "Amy, do you want to stay with me?"

"Yes," I said. "I hate my cousin Jessica," I added. I didn't say anything about my father because it would just make my mother mad again.

My mother giggled. Liz giggled. Then they both laughed so hard that the man at the next table looked at them.

My mother put her hand on my arm. "Liz and I talked, Amy. She thinks it would work out."

Liz nodded, smiling. But she looked kind of worried, too.

So it was all fixed. I'd stay with Liz. I decided to take my favorite tapes for the VCR—and Pink, of course. I told him about it when we got home.

"You'll like the city, Pink," I said, opening his cage. I held his warm body in my hands. "You'll have your same home, just like here, but when you look out the window, you'll see these big buildings. And maybe, maybe I'll take you to the park someday."

Pink kissed my cheek with his warm pink nose.

"I won't tell my father I'm going to be in the city all summer till I get there, Pink. It'll be a surprise. He'll be glad."

Of course, I thought, my father was always busy painting. But he would make time for me, because he loved me. I was sure about that. Almost.

Chapter Two

took the train to the city the same day my mother flew to Africa. She drove me to the station.

"It's only three months," she said.

From the train, I could see her standing in the parking lot, waving. Three months was a long time. And she couldn't even call.

Pink went with me in a box with holes. I carried his cage in a bag.

I went to Penn Station, which is where I go

when I visit my father. I don't like Penn Station. It's too big and there are lots and lots of people. They all walk very fast.

Liz met me at the station. "What's that?" she asked, pointing at the box with holes.

"Pink. My white rat. He has pink eyes and a pink nose."

"A rat! Does it stay in a cage?"

"Sure."

Actually, Pink doesn't like to stay in his cage. He likes to run around my room and do things. He's very smart.

Liz grabbed my suitcase. She walked very fast, just like the people in the station. Her sandals went slap, slap, slap on the ground. It was hard to keep up with her. When we got outside, she stepped off the curb and waved her arm for a taxicab. Two of them went right by her.

"Darn! Let's walk to the corner." But just then a taxi stopped in front of us.

When we were inside, I could tell Pink was worried. The box he was in was shaking.

"It'll be okay," I told him. "It's not a long ride."

We went up a wide street with tall buildings and then down a narrow street with shorter buildings. The taxi stopped in front of the big old red building I remembered.

Slap, slap, slap. Liz was practically running into the building. "Hi, Howie," she said loudly as we went by an old man sitting on a sofa in the lobby. His eyes were closed.

"Uh, oh!" The old man, who was wearing a brown uniform and a brown hat, jumped up and got to the elevators just before Liz did. "Number eight!" he said, waving his hand in the air and then pushing the elevator button.

Liz smiled. "This is Amy, Howie. She'll be staying with me this summer."

"And where are you from, young lady?" asked Howie, bending down so he could look into my face.

"Lordsville, New Jersey."

"I was in New Jersey once," said Howie.

Crash! The elevator door opened and we got on.

Clank! Creak! The elevator went up very slowly.

"You have to be very careful with this elevator, Amy," said Liz. "It's old and they don't maintain it right. Now if it stops between floors, you press this button here marked Alarm."

"What happens then?"

"The bell rings and the repairman comes. It's only happened to me once. But ever since then, I've never gotten in the elevator without something to read." Liz opened her shoulder purse and showed me a paperback book.

Crash! It was the eighth floor.

As soon as we reached Liz's door, a dog inside started barking.

"I don't think you've met Maud, Amy. I got her last winter." When Liz opened the door, a little dog with curly gray hair was jumping all around inside. Then she saw me.

"Grrrrrrrrrr," said the dog.

"Maud!" said Liz. "Be nice. Amy is going to stay here for a while."

I walked inside and Maud sniffed my leg. "Grrrrr," she said again. I held Pink's box up in the air and walked around Maud.

"I'm afraid Maud isn't used to children," said Liz. "She hardly ever sees any."

Liz's apartment had a big living room and a big bedroom, a little tiny kitchen and a long skinny bathroom, and a wide place in the hall with a desk.

"I work here in the hall," said Liz. "It would be great to have two bedrooms, but I just can't afford it." She was walking down the hall to the bedroom as she talked. "I'm putting your suitcase in the bedroom, Amy. That'll be your room. I'll sleep on the sofa bed in the living room."

I followed her into the bedroom. It had one big window. Right across from it was the window of another apartment. I put Pink's box on top of a high chest of drawers. Then I took the cage out of the bag and put it on the chest, too.

"Now you can go back home," I said. I pulled the tape off the box and lifted Pink out with both hands.

"Grrrrrrr!" Maud was right behind me, staring at Pink!

I quickly put Pink in his cage and closed the cage door tight.

Maud put both paws on the chest and looked up at Pink. Pink got down on the floor of his cage and shook harder than ever.

Liz came over to the chest and looked at Pink. "Is it cold?"

"Nervous. He doesn't like to travel. And he isn't used to dogs."

Liz opened the bottom two drawers of the chest. They were empty. "You can have these, and half the closet there. Why don't you unpack and settle in while I go start dinner?"

Her sandals went slap, slap, slap along the hall to the kitchen. Maud followed her. I heard pots and pans being moved around.

I got out my VCR tapes and a drawing pad my father gave me and put them on a table. I decided to put my clothes away later. Then I went into the living room. There was a big window there, but all you could see from it was roofs. I went all around the room, touching things. Maud watched me from the hall.

I hadn't noticed it before, but Liz's whole apartment was just full of little things. There were vases and rocks and shells and pictures and statues and a couple of things I didn't recognize.

On the table next to the sofa was the head of a man with a beard. And next to him was a statue of a woman in a long dress. Her dress was pink and her hair was yellow.

I touched the woman's hair.

"That's Maud," said Liz. She was standing outside the kitchen, stirring something.

"I thought the dog was Maud."

"The statue is Maud and the dog is Maud, too. I like the name Maud."

Liz put down the bowl and crossed her hands on her blouse. She closed her eyes. " 'Come into the garden, Maud, for the black bat, night, has flown,' " she said in a loud voice. She opened her eyes. "Alfred, Lord Tennyson. He wrote a poem about Maud. The man's head is a bust of Alfred, Lord Tennyson. I bought it in England, and I bought the statue on the same trip, so I call it Maud."

Something went ding in the kitchen and Liz went back inside.

I'd never heard of Alfred, Lord Tennyson. Or anybody named Maud. And now I'd met two Mauds in one day.

I kept moving around the living room, looking at things. There were a lot of things there but one thing was missing. I hadn't seen it in the bedroom, either.

I went to the door of the kitchen.

"Grrrrrrr," growled Maud the dog. She was sitting in front of the door.

"Liz—do you have a TV?"

"Uh-huh. In the armoire."

"The what?"

"The big cupboard in the living room."

The armoire had a stuffed bird in a glass jar on top of it. I opened the doors. There it was! But it was awfully small. I switched it on.

The picture was black and white! Not only that, but it was full of snow. I hadn't seen such an awful picture since the time the tree fell on our antenna. I looked around. Of course there wasn't any VCR, either!

I went back into the bedroom and closed the door. I picked up a tape: "The Weerd Family at the Beach." It was one of my favorites. I played it every week, practically. But now I wouldn't be able to play it for three months!

Poor Pink wasn't shaking as much as before, but he didn't look happy.

"I don't like it here so much, either," I said.

Ring!

I could hear Liz talking. Then her footsteps came down the hall. "It's your mother, Amy," called Liz. "She's at the airport."

"Amy? Is everything okay?"

"Sure." I couldn't tell her about the VCR with Liz right there.

"Remember, it's only three months."

"That's a long time."

"I love you and don't you forget it," she said.

"I love you too."

When I hung up I felt like she was already in Africa. I picked up the phone again and dialed my father's number. But he didn't answer. Lots of times he doesn't answer the phone because he's painting.

"Amy?" Liz was standing there, carrying a leash, a stick and a paper bag. "Let's take Maud for a walk while the meat is cooking."

Maud was jumping all around again.

"You can carry this bag," said Liz as we went out the door.

"What's it for?"

But Liz was rushing down the hall toward the elevators. I wondered if she had her book somewhere.

"I think something's wrong with the TV," I said as we went clanking down.

"Oh, it works," said Liz. "I was just watching the news last night."

"It's all full of snow," I said as we went through the lobby, but Liz was so far ahead of me she didn't hear. In a chair, Howie had his eyes closed.

Liz had stopped in front of a shop. "Look at that adorable teapot," she was saying. "It's so Victorian. But I've spent too much this month already."

"Why don't you get a color TV?" I asked. "And a VCR?"

"I don't watch TV that much," said Liz. "I read a lot. There's a library nearby. I'll take you! We can get lots of children's books there."

"I don't like to read," I said.

"You . . . don't . . . like . . . to . . . read!" Liz was staring at me like I was some horrible monster or something. "But Amy, what are you going to do in the apartment all day if you don't read?"

"I don't know," I said. I hadn't thought about that. No TV! And I didn't have any friends in the city. The three months stretched ahead of me like forever.

"We'll move the TV into the bedroom," said Liz. "Then you can watch it whenever you want."

I stared at the sidewalk. At my horrible cousin Jessica's, they had three color TVs and two VCRs. The VCR had this thing where you could take out the commercials. And one of the TVs had a giant screen, almost like a movie screen.

Liz had stopped again. She was scooping something off the pavement with the stick she was carrying. "Open the bag," she said.

"Huh?"

Liz was putting something gooey and smelly in the bag. It was dog poop! I remembered then that there was some kind of law in New York where you had to pick up dog poop. I scrunched the top of the bag closed as quick as I could.

"What do I do with this?"

"Carry it home and put it in the incinerator."

I held the bag away from me. Dog poop is so disgusting, not like rat poop.

"Tomorrow you can walk Maud around the block by yourself," said Liz. "Here's how to use the scooper." She slid the stick along the pavement and picked up a stone. "Okay?"

Yuck! "Okay."

Just before we got back to Liz's apartment house, we went by a little store. On the front was a big sign that said: PIZZA.

"I like pizza," I said. "Let's get some for dinner."

"Oh, no," said Liz. "I've made a lovely ragout for us."

"What's that?"

"A beef stew," said Liz, moving ahead of me. "It has leeks and scallions and kohlrabi . . ."

"I don't like any of those things," I said. "I don't even know what they are." But she was so far ahead of me by then that she didn't hear me, of course.

I tripped over a piece of sidewalk that was sticking up and almost fell down. This was a terrible place. I didn't like the food. I didn't like Maud. I didn't like the apartment. I didn't like Liz, either. She didn't pay any attention to me. She walked too fast. She recited poetry.

And there wasn't anything to do in the whole place but look at that awful black-and-white TV. Even if I got to see my father more, it wouldn't be worth it!

There was a phone booth on the corner, just before you got to Liz's building. When Liz was busy I would go out and call my aunt, my horrible cousin Jessica's mother. I would ask if I could spend the summer there. I wouldn't even bother to call my father. He'd never know I'd almost been in the city all summer. He'd never know he could have seen me every week, or even more.

"Amy!" Liz had finally noticed I wasn't with her and was waiting for me.

In the lobby, Howie was still sitting in the chair, head down and eyes closed. Maud put her paws on his knees.

"Uh! Oh!" He jumped up. But this time Liz got to the button first. She pushed it, smiling. I guessed maybe they were having some kind of a race.

Howie bent down to look at me. "And how do you like our city, young lady?"

"It's okay."

"The finest city in the world," said Howie, nodding. "Why, I wouldn't live anywhere else!"

Crash! The elevator door opened and a girl a little taller than me got out. She looked at me and smiled. I smiled back, holding the bag behind me.

"Hi, Ms. Farrelly."

Liz drew in her breath. "We can't eat that every night."

"Why not?"

Liz's face got the look again. Then it went away, like she had ironed her face.

"We've got to negotiate, Amy."

"What's that?"

"I'll give you something you want and you give me something I want. What if you eat my dinners six times a week and we go to a McFry's the other night?"

I thought. "What if I eat your dinners three nights and we go to McFry's the other nights?"

Finally we negotiated a settlement. I would eat her dinners five times a week and we would go to McFry's the other nights. And no French food. I felt so good about the settlement that I ate some of the ragout. I was hungry.

After dinner I called my father again. The phone rang and rang. I was just putting it down when a voice said: "Hello."

"It's me, Daddy!"

"Daddy? Who's that calling me Daddy?"

"Oh, Daddy! I called you this afternoon. You didn't answer."

"I was finishing a painting, Tulip. Are you in Lordsville?"

He always calls me Tulip, but I forget why. "No! I'm here, in the city! I'll be here all summer, while

Mother's in Africa! I'm staying with Liz!"

"Liz? Who's Liz?"

"My godmother Liz."

"Oh, *that* Liz. All summer, did you say?"

I thought he'd be glad I would be there all summer, but he didn't sound glad. He didn't sound anything. Maybe he was thinking about his painting. Once he was thinking about his painting so much he forgot I was coming to see him. I waited in Penn Station for two hours because he didn't answer his phone.

"Well, why don't you and Godmother Liz come down here tomorrow afternoon?" my father was saying. "There's a craft show in the park. Then we can have dinner."

I would see him the next day!

Liz couldn't go to the craft show but she said she'd join us for dinner. So the next afternoon, right after lunch, I went to my father's apartment by myself in a taxi. Howie called the taxi. He went out in front of the building under the torn canopy and whistled very loud. It worked. A taxi came right away.

"Take care of this young lady," said Howie to the driver. "She's from New Jersey."

"I was in New Jersey once," said the driver to me as we drove away.

Liz lives uptown and my father lives downtown. She lives on the East Side and he lives on the West

Side. So the taxi had to go down and then across to get to my father's apartment building. It didn't take so long because it was Sunday and there wasn't much traffic.

My father lives in this big square building that takes up a whole block right next to the river. It used to be an office building but now everybody who lives in it is an artist. They don't pay much rent because the city runs the building.

My father was standing right outside on the sidewalk, waiting for me.

"Hello, Tulip." He hugged me and then he stood back and looked at me very hard. Nobody else looks at me like that, not even my mother.

"You look good," he said.

My father isn't tall and he isn't short and he's kind of thin and he has brown hair. He says you wouldn't notice him in a crowd. I look more like him than like my mother.

After he paid the driver, we went inside. I like his building because it's so strange. Artists need lots of room for their work, so the apartments don't have ordinary walls. Instead they have these walls you push around on wheels to wherever you want them.

His apartment is on the third floor. We rode up on the big elevator. It's big because people carry paintings and sculpture up and down in it.

"How are you and the Godmother hitting it off?"

"Okay." I looked at the floor and sighed.

"You sure?"

"She makes this funny food. And she only has a black-and-white TV."

My father smiled, patting my shoulder. "Could be worse, Tulip." We got off the elevator and walked down the hall. My father opened the apartment door and we went inside. "I haven't seen Liz for years. Is she still pretty?"

"She's not as pretty as Mother!"

"No woman's as pretty as your mother. She's beautiful. And brilliant. Trouble is, no one can live with her," said my father.

"*I* live with her."

"That's different," he said. "I mean no man can live with her."

"A man wants to," I said.

"Do you like him?"

"No. He never looks at me."

"A bad sign. Hold out, Tulip, hold out for the best."

"You're the best." I looked up at him.

He *is* the best. The ones who are in love with my mother now say these dumb things and never make me laugh. They don't really look at me, either, and they want to be alone with my mother all the time.

"Your mother and I will never get back together," he said. "You know that, don't you?"

"Yes," I whispered. My mother said the same thing. And whenever my mother and father saw each other, they fought.

My father squeezed my shoulder. "How do you like the new painting?" he asked, pointing.

My father's apartment is like one big room because he doesn't use the walls on wheels. Most of what's in the room are paintings. He paints trees—big, big pictures of trees. He used to paint red trees and blue trees and yellow trees. I like his green trees the best. He painted a little picture of a green tree just for me. It's in my bedroom at home.

The new painting was standing up against the table. It was purple.

"It looks like you're standing in a forest, a forest of purple trees."

He hugged me hard. "That's one of the best things I've heard lately. How about a Coke?"

He got us both a Coke and we sat on an old sofa in the corner. It's the only furniture except for the big table all covered with paints. There were piles of newspapers and magazines on the floor.

"I just sold a painting," said my father.

"A big one?"

"A very big one. To the Waugh Corporation. They're going to put it in their boardroom. My gallery is in heaven."

He swept his hand around the room. "It's paid most of my rent for a year. And something else. Look behind the purple tree."

On a little table was a color TV!

"Used," said my father. "But a good one."

"Gosh!" I switched it on. The picture was good. "Liz's TV doesn't even work right." I went over and stood next to my father. "She doesn't have a VCR, either. And she has this mean little dog, Maud."

"A dog called Maud!" My father shook his head. "Is there anything good there?"

"There's a girl my age who lives in the building."

"If it gets too bad, you can always camp out here, for a night or two. I've still got the sleeping bag."

I took a deep breath. "Can I stay here all summer?"

"No!" he said, very quick. "You'd be bored here."

"I'll watch TV!"

"All day? This place is too small for both of us, Amy."

My father's apartment was too small for me. Africa was too hot and buggy for me. All of a sudden, I felt like I was all alone in the whole world, even though I was standing right next to my father. A lump came up in my throat.

"I've got to concentrate on painting," said my

father in a hard voice. It was the voice he uses with my mother. He got up and walked over to the purple tree. "It's good," he said. "I *know* it's good." He turned around. "Let's go to the craft show."

I swallowed but only part of the lump went away. "Okay."

My father held my hand as we walked along the street and told me a funny story about a fat lady artist who lived in his building. He looked down at me and smiled and then it was like there was nobody else in the whole world, just the two of us, even though we were walking along the street with all these people on it.

The craft show was in Washington Square Park. There were people selling pottery and wooden boxes and silver jewelry and lots of other things. It was so crowded it was hard to walk down the aisles.

"Let's visit booth number forty-two," said my father, looking at a program.

Booth number forty-two had clothes hanging all over it. All the clothes looked the same except that they came in different colors. A woman with long red hair was helping another woman try on a jacket. The woman with red hair smiled at us.

The woman in the jacket turned around in front of a mirror.

"I love it!" She started looking in her purse for her money.

Behind her back, my father put his hands together over his head and shook them.

When the woman walked away with her jacket, my father introduced me to the red-haired woman. "This is Janine, Amy. She's a very talented weaver. And a friend."

Janine smiled again with lots of white teeth. She was pretty, but not as pretty as my mother. "Hello, Amy. You look like your father."

"How's business?" asked my father.

"Good." They stood there smiling at each other. Then Janine looked at me. "I have some small things, Amy. Let's see . . ."

She picked something yellow out of a pile on a table. "Let's try this on."

The yellow thing looked like a rug. There was a hideous red bird flying across one part of the rug.

"It goes on like this," said Janine, pulling it over my head. "It's a poncho. The Fumalee Indians wear them when it rains. This red bird is the rain god. When the poncho gets wet, you just squeeze out the water. Look in the mirror."

The yellow rug hung down to my knees. The bird covered my whole chest. I could just see myself wearing it to the Farragut Elementary School in Lordsville. "Excuse me while I squeeze out my poncho." All this water would come out and run over the floor.

"Keep it, Amy," said Janine. "A little gift from Janine Creations."

"No," said my father. "I know how much you charge for these, Janine."

Janine put her hand on my father's chest and smiled at him. "My treat," she said.

She took the yellow thing off and put it in a bag. "I know we're going to be great friends," she said softly, her hand on my shoulder. She handed me the bag.

After we left booth number forty-two we walked up and down the aisles, looking at the crafts. My father talked about how talented Janine was, how she had won this fellowship to study weaving with the Fumalees in South America after she graduated from college and how now she had an apartment in the same building he did.

"It's more crowded than mine," said my father. "She has two looms the size of grand pianos. We have to eat on the floor, like a picnic."

Why was my father talking so much about Janine? Maybe he was in love with her! Maybe he was going to let her stay in the apartment even though he wouldn't let me! With her looms, there wouldn't be any room for me at all. And Janine would give me these horrible woven clothes I'd have to wear.

"You look funny," said my father. "Do you feel all right?"

"Yes." But I didn't. I felt alone again, right in the middle of the craft fair.

"Well, I think we've seen enough," said my father. "Let's go back to the apartment."

On the way out, we passed a booth that sold ice-cream cones. They had some funny flavors like iced tea, tomato, and hot-hot.

"Can I have a hot-hot cone?"

The hot-hot cone was orange and tasted like cold chili. It was good.

We walked slowly back to the apartment. "Do you think the Godmother will go into shock when she sees my apartment?" asked my father.

"Maybe. She's very neat. All her magazines are in a magazine rack. All her books are in a bookcase."

My father groaned. "Anything else?"

"She makes the bed as soon as she gets up. She does the dishes right after she eats."

"Stop! Stop!" He put his hands to his head.

I giggled. My father could always make me laugh. "Maybe we ought to clean up," I said.

"That's a very good idea, Tulip."

When we got to his apartment, he pushed a wall on wheels in front of the big table. We pushed the paints to one side of the table and piled most of the magazines and newspapers on it. Then he did the dishes in the sink.

While he was doing that, I took the bag with the

poncho and pushed it under the sofa.

"How does it look?" asked my father, looking around after he was finished with the dishes.

"It's better."

"I've got a tray somewhere." He opened a cabinet in the kitchen.

The doorbell rang.

I pressed the buzzer to let Liz in the front door. Soon we could hear her sandals slap, slap, slapping down the hall.

My father opened the door.

"Carl!"

"Liz!"

"You're as pretty as ever."

"Oh, Carl! You look the same, too."

"Come into my magnificent parlor, Liz. Cocktail?"

"Do you have white wine?"

While my father was getting Liz some white wine, Liz asked me about the craft show. But I don't think she listened to what I said. All the time I was talking she kept sneaking these little looks around. At first I thought she was looking at the mess, but then I saw she wasn't looking at the room. She was looking at the paintings.

"Excuse me, Amy."

Liz got up and walked around, stopping in front of the purple trees.

My father came back with a tray with a plate of cheese and some glasses on it.

"Carl—I had no idea. These are superb! The colors. The depth. The movement."

My father stood there holding the tray. "You like them?"

"I love them!"

"I think you mean it." They stood next to each other, looking at the purple trees.

"Late evening," said Liz in a dreamy voice. "After the sun goes down but before the moon comes up."

"That's how I felt when I did it."

"Carl—are you selling?"

"Not much. Art's more than painting, you know."

Liz nodded. "I know. So is writing. The things I do to sell my work . . ."

"I'm not good at that sort of thing," said my father.

I looked out the window. There was a tugboat on the river, pushing a long, low boat. Liz laughed at something my father said. They seemed to like each other, I thought. That was funny, because my father was so messy and Liz was so neat. And she liked nice furniture and he didn't care. And she . . .

"Ha, ha, ha, ha, ha, hahaha," laughed Liz again,

throwing her head back. And my father laughed, too, but not so much. Yes, they definitely looked like they liked each other. I will never understand grown-ups, even if I live to be very old.

We went to dinner at this Mexican restaurant my father took me to before because, he said, it's cheap but has lots of atmosphere. I had tacos and guacamole salad. It's the only salad I eat because it isn't like a salad.

My father told us a funny story about how the income tax people called and he had to take his records down there but they couldn't read them because they were all covered with paint. We all laughed a lot and my father looked very happy. It was fun being with my father and Liz for dinner, I thought.

"Near Liz's there's this place that sells pizza," I told my father. "Will you take us there?"

My father held up his hand. "I promise. Next weekend."

"Oh, Carl, that isn't really a good pizza place," said Liz. "Why don't you come to dinner next weekend? I'll show you my log. It's not that hard to keep track of your expenses."

We went home by subway. "I didn't realize, Amy, that your father's paintings were so good," said Liz. "He's a real artist. When did he start painting seriously?"

I tried to remember. He fixed up the attic in the

New Jersey house as a studio. It was messy, like his apartment. I got his green paint in my hair. "I was real little," I said. "It was when I started school."

"He should be selling more," said Liz. "It's so hard to make it as an artist. Or a writer."

It was our stop.

Going down the street, Liz said: "Oh, I forgot to tell you, Amy. Matilda came by. She'll be back tomorrow."

Matilda!

Chapter Four

◆

L iz was dusting her computer when I went into the hall the next morning. "Breakfast's on the table," she said without looking at me. She sat right down at the computer and started hitting the keys very fast.

"You go to work *early*," I said, but she didn't even answer. It was like she was a whole different person than the person she'd been the night before.

I went over to the table. The breakfast was orange juice, this awful cereal called Miles O'Fiber that I saw on TV, and a muffin. I bit into the muffin. Blueberry. It was good.

When I finished the muffin, I went back into the bedroom and turned on the black-and-white TV. When would Matilda come? It seemed like forever until the doorbell rang.

Maud started barking, and I heard Liz say a bad word. Maybe that was Matilda! I opened the bedroom door.

Liz was looking through the little window in the top of the door. "Where . . . ? Oh—Matilda!"

Matilda! I dashed to the door as Liz pulled it open.

"Hi, Ms. Farrelly. Hi, Amy. Hi, Maud." Matilda looked at the computer. "Are you writing, Ms. Farrelly?"

Liz nodded. "I'm having a problem with my novel. How are you, Matilda?" But she was looking at the computer again, not Matilda. She sat down. "Why don't you take Matilda to your room, Amy?"

I closed the door to the bedroom behind us before Maud could get in.

"My mother says writers are in another world when they're working," said Matilda. She looked around the room. "Is that a *rat?*"

"Yes. His name is Pink."

"It's kind of pretty."

"Would you like to hold him?"

"I don't know. A rat!" Matilda looked nervous.

I opened the cage door and lifted Pink out. I put his warm body in Matilda's lap.

"Oh!" said Matilda. She touched Pink. "It's smooth!" She patted Pink's back.

We sat on the bed. "You can put him down," I said. "Pink won't go off the bed if I'm here."

Matilda opened her hands. Pink walked slowly across the bedspread, whiskers twitching.

"It's really cute," said Matilda. She looked at me. "Why are you staying here this summer?"

I told her.

"Are your parents divorced?"

"Yes."

"So are mine! I live with my mother and my sister."

Pink had climbed onto my lap. Matilda reached over to pet him again. "This bedroom is just like mine," she said. "But mine has twin beds because I share it with my little sister. Do you know we have the only two-bedroom apartment in the whole building?"

Matilda's voice told me this was something special but it didn't seem so special to me. In Lordsville, just about everyone has at least two bedrooms, and lots of people have more. "The reason why," went on Matilda, "is that a long time ago, before we even lived here, somebody took the one-room apartment next door and made it part of ours. Now my mother uses it as her office. She sleeps there, too. She's a literary agent."

"What's that?"

"It's a person who sells people's books to publishers," said Matilda. She sounded surprised.

"Are those your VCR tapes?" she asked, pointing to my "Weerd Family" tapes.

"Yes. But I can't play them because Liz doesn't have a VCR. Do you have one?

"No," said Matilda. "We have a television but we can only watch at it one hour a day unless it's a special program. My mother thinks people shouldn't watch television too much. Because if they do, she can't sell so many books."

Matilda lowered her voice. "Can you keep a secret?"

"Of course!"

"I watch 'Los Angeles Emergency' practically every day, right here in the building!" She giggled, clapping her hands over her mouth.

"Where? Do you have a friend in the building? 'Los Angeles Emergency' is my favorite soap! Paverly Yard, my favorite actress, is in it!"

"Oh, Paverly Yard! I love her! No, I don't have any friends in the building. As soon as the kids get older, people move. The apartments are too small. My best friend moved to Great Neck last year."

"My best friend moved to Scottsdale, Arizona, last year."

We looked at each other, nodding. Matilda was

like me, I thought, even though she was all excited about two bedrooms and her mother was a literary agent.

Matilda lowered her voice again. "Meet me in the lobby at two forty-five today, like we were going for a walk. I'll show you where I watch 'Los Angeles Emergency!' "

"Okay!"

Matilda looked at a big watch on her wrist. The watch face was the face of a pig and a pink plastic strap held it on her wrist. "I'm taking my tap dancing lesson at the Y this morning," said Matilda. "I've got to go. Do you tap?"

"No."

"I just love it. I'll show you a step later. I can't do it here because my mother says I can't tap over anyone's head."

When we went to the door, Liz was staring at her computer. She waved but she didn't look up.

I guess that was about the most boring morning I ever spent. I watched the black-and-white TV and I drew a picture of a pigeon that sat on the windowsill. I was actually glad when Liz asked me to take Maud around the block.

Howie was sleeping when Maud and I went by. We walked slowly around the block. It was a lot more interesting than walking in Lordsville because here you could look in the store windows, and there were always lots of funny-looking people on the street. In Lordsville, everybody looks the same.

When Maud did her poop, I scooped it up very fast, looking around to see if anybody was watching. But you know what? Nobody was! They didn't seem to care at all. In Lordsville, people watch you.

Howie was awake when we got back. He gave Maud and me a piece of hard candy.

"Thank you," I said, even though I don't like that kind of candy.

"Miss Farrelly, she doesn't like for Maud to have candy," said Howie. "But she likes it, see?"

Maud was trying to chew the candy, making all these funny movements with her jaws. But her tail was wagging.

Well, you can believe that at 2:30 I was back in the lobby, waiting for Matilda. I sat beside Howie on one of the sofas. They were metal, like the kind people use outdoors, and they were chained to the walls.

"Why are the sofas chained to the walls?" I asked.

When Howie wasn't sleeping, he was very friendly. "We used to have real sofas," he said. "With upholstery! They reupholstered them every other year right up till the sixties. But then it changed. The upholstery, it got all dirty and they didn't reupholster any more. And then one night, when the night doorman was downstairs in the basement, someone stole those sofas! Took them clean away!"

"They must've had a truck," I said.

"You better believe it! So after that, the management got these metal sofas and chained them to the wall. They're not too comfortable." Howie moved around a little on the sofa. Then he took off his hat to scratch his head. His hair was all white. Howie must be very, very old, I thought.

Howie told me about some of the people in the building, like Tom Tyrell, who is an actor, and Mrs. Goldman, who is the mother of a lawyer who owns two Mercedes-Benz cars.

"One is gray, and the other one is blue," said Howie. "He gives me twenty dollars every time he comes, just to watch the car."

Crash! The elevator door opened. "Hi!" said Matilda. She went sideways across the lobby floor, making little movements with her feet. "This is the step we learned today. It's the same one Ruby Keeler did in *Dames*."

"Who's Ruby Keeler?" I asked.

"She was this tap dancer a long, long time ago in the movies," said Matilda. "We saw some of her movies at the Tap Extravaganza."

"I saw Ruby Keeler once in person," said Eddie. "That was a dancer!"

"She was fast," said Matilda, moving around us.

"I'll show you some more steps in the basement, Amy. Come on."

"The basement?"

Matilda was already dancing through a door next to the elevator. I followed her down a flight of cement steps.

"I wish I could dance down steps," said Matilda. "But I'm not ready for it yet."

At the bottom of the steps was a wide hall. Matilda tapped down the hall. "Of course I don't have my taps on," she said. "So it doesn't sound right. Now here's an easy step."

Matilda moved her feet slowly back and forth. I did the same thing.

"That's right. Now you have to practice it until you can do it fast." She looked at her pig watch. "It's almost three!"

Matilda ran down the hall with me after her. She went around a corner and through an open door. The door led into a big room. Two men sat in chairs at one end of the room in front of a huge color TV set. There were some empty chairs next to them.

"Here she is," said one of the men.

"Hi, Al, hi, John," said Matilda, out of breath. "This is Amy. She's staying with Ms. Farrelly in 8-J. Amy, this is Al, our super, and John, our night doorman. Amy's from New Jersey."

The men smiled at us. "I was in New Jersey once," said John, the old, thin one.

"My cousin moved to New Jersey," said Al, the middle-aged, fat one.

There was the sound of a siren on the TV and the words "Los Angeles Emergency" came on the screen.

I was really glad we didn't miss this day's program. Because this was the day Paverly Yard, who plays Gillian, the head nurse, discovered that the patient who was in a coma in intensive care was her husband, who disappeared a year ago.

"That was so exciting," said Matilda when the credits started rolling on the screen. "Oh, I hope Eric gets better! Then he and Paverly can get back together."

"But maybe he disappeared on purpose," I said. "I don't trust him."

"I do," said Matilda. "You know the way I found out Al and John watch 'Los Angeles Emergency'? I was practicing my tap steps in the basement so I wouldn't be dancing over anyone's head. And I heard the 'Los Angeles Emergency' theme song! I used to watch it at my best friend's apartment."

"She came running in here, all excited," said Al.

A phone rang on a desk in the corner. In back of the desk was a Peg-Board with all kinds of tools. Al picked up the phone. "Yes, Mrs. Goldman." He listened. "Sorry, I don't have the time today. Maybe I can squeeze it in tomorrow." He put down the phone.

A game show was on the screen. Al sat down in front of the set again.

"How's the dancing coming, Matilda?" asked John.

"This is the step I learned today," said Matilda. She moved across the room. "Ruby Keeler did it in *Dames,*" she called from the end of the room.

"She was a cute one," said John. "You remind me of her, Amy."

"I do?" I had never heard of Ruby Keeler before today. Was I cute? Nobody ever said so in Lordsville.

Matilda came tapping back. "Let's go up to my apartment, Amy. I want to tell you about this book I'm reading. It's so great."

I didn't tell her I didn't like to read.

Matilda's apartment was just like Liz's except that there was this extra door in the hall once you got inside. The door was open and through it we could hear a woman's voice.

"No, Dorothy, I haven't heard from Mac-Crowells yet. I just sent your manuscript to them five days ago!"

"My mom," said Matilda, as we walked down the hall to the bedroom. "She's working."

I wished my mother worked at home. I wished my mother was with me, instead of thousands of miles away.

Matilda opened the bedroom door. "My sister's

at camp," she said, "so I have my room all to myself."

Matilda's room was just like Liz's except that there were two of everything. Two beds, two dressers, two chairs, two desks, two bookcases. I knew which was Matilda's side because there were photographs of people pinned all over the wall and some of them were tap dancing.

"Is Ruby Keeler here?" I asked.

"Sure." Matilda pointed to a photograph of a girl with short hair and big eyes. She wore a sailor hat. She was very pretty.

"You know," said Matilda, "you do look kind of like her. Stand next to the picture."

I stood next to it.

"Yes!" said Matilda. "You do!"

"Do I?" I felt happy. At home, people always said, "You don't look very much like your mother." It made me feel ugly when they said that, because she's so beautiful. But Ruby Keeler was pretty, so maybe I was, too! I looked at the photograph again. There was a date in one corner. 1933. 1933!

"Ruby Keeler is an old lady!" I said.

"In her movies, she's young," said Matilda. She took a book from the table between the two beds. "Here's that book. It's about this girl who lived a long time ago who goes to this huge house with a walled garden. I've read it twice already—it's absolutely my favorite book! When I finish it, I could take it out of the library for you."

I put my hands straight down at my sides. "I don't read books unless I have to. I don't like to read."

Matilda sat down on the bed with the book. "You don't read anything?"

"Only in school."

Matilda put the book back on the table. Then she looked up at me. "How long have your parents been divorced?"

"Three years."

"It's four for mine. And my father got married again."

"Do you like her?"

"Well, I don't like her a *lot*. She tries to be friends. She tries too hard. You know what I mean?"

I told her about Janine. "She gave me this woven poncho like the Indians in South America wear. It's yellow and has this big red bird on the shoulder."

"It sounds awful!"

"It is!"

The phone rang. "That's the home phone, not the office phone," said Matilda. She dashed out the door.

"Hello. Yes, Ms. Farrelly. I'll get her."

Matilda handed me the phone, her eyes very big.

"Something's happened," she whispered.

"Oh, Amy," came Liz's voice over the phone. "Pink has disappeared!"

We didn't wait for the elevator. We ran up the steps to the eighth floor. Liz was in the apartment doorway, holding a cloth. She started talking as I ran toward the bedroom. "I was stuck on my problem," she said. "So I started dusting the bedroom. I picked up Pink's cage. Maud got all excited and jumped on me. I dropped the cage! The door came open! And Pink just disappeared! I've looked everywhere!"

I ran into the bedroom, Matilda and Liz behind me. The cage still lay on the floor. Maud was sniffing it.

"Maud ate Pink!" I cried. "And you let her!"

"No, no!" said Liz. "She couldn't have! There would be fur or something left!"

"Maud's a murderer!" I yelled. I threw myself on the bed, crying. Pink, my beautiful soft warm Pink, was dead.

Chapter Five

◆

As soon as I woke up the next day, I remembered. Pink! I started crying again. I loved Pink so much. It was Liz's fault he'd gotten eaten by Maud. I hated Maud, and Liz, too. My mother wouldn't have dusted Pink's cage. She never dusted anything.

I got dressed and opened the bedroom door. Liz was sitting at her desk, looking at her computer. As soon as I came out, she turned around.

"Oh, Amy, I am sorry."

I walked by her to the table without saying a single word. There were two muffins on the table but no Miles O'Fiber. I sat down.

"And Maud is sorry, too," said Liz.

Maud the dog came up to me and sat on her hind legs with her paws up. "Murderer!" I whispered. Liz heard me. "I'm sure Maud didn't hurt Pink," she said. "She just frightened him."

I bit into a blueberry muffin. Maud put down her paws and lay down under Liz's desk.

Liz sighed so loud I could her her all the way across the room. Then she turned back to her computer. *Click! Click! Clickety clickety click!*

Matilda was going to be home this morning. So right after breakfast, I said, "I'm going to Matilda's" and slammed the apartment door behind me fast.

Matilda opened her door. "Is Pink still gone?" she asked right away.

I nodded. We went into Matilda's room and sat on her bed. "If Liz weren't so clean," I said, "she wouldn't have been dusting Pink's cage and she wouldn't have dropped it and Maud wouldn't have eaten him. It's Liz's fault!"

"Is she that clean?" asked Matilda.

"Well, she dusts her computer every morning. And she vacuums the rug every day."

Matilda looked impressed. "That is clean. But

you know, I don't think Maud ate Pink. I think Pink ran away because Maud scared him."

"Last night I looked everywhere in the apartment," I said. "Even in back of the radiators. And I put out some crackers and peanut butter in my room. That's Pink's favorite food. But it was still there in the morning."

"I think Pink ran out of the apartment," said Matilda. "He's probably hiding somewhere in the building. I know! Let's put up a 'Lost' sign! We can offer a reward!"

It couldn't hurt to put up a sign, I thought. "Okay. My mother gave me some money when she left. Do you think twenty dollars is a good reward?"

"Twenty dollars! That's a great reward!"

Matilda took some colored paper and a marking pen out of her desk. She sat down in the desk chair. "Now what'll we say?" She scrunched up her face. "How's this? 'Reward! Lost white rat. See apartment 8-J.'"

"I can draw a picture of Pink," I said.

"Can you? Oh good." Matilda scrunched up her face again and began lettering. Then she stopped. "I'm running out of room." She took another piece of paper, an orange piece.

"Use pink," I said. "It'll be like Pink's name. And we'll say, 'Answers to name of Pink.'"

"Does Pink know his name?"

"I think so. He always looks at me when I call him."

Matilda took a piece of pink paper out of the pile and began lettering again. After a while, she held the sign up. It looked very nice.

"You can draw Pink at the bottom," said Matilda.

"I'll need a pencil," I said. "With an eraser."

Matilda gave me a pencil with a big eraser. I drew Pink's round shape in the empty space at the bottom. I put in his cute pink ears and his long whiskers and his little pink feet.

Tears started falling on the paper. Drawing Pink's picture made me feel worse.

"Oh, Amy," said Matilda. "I like Pink, too. He's very nice for a rat."

I took the pen and drew over the penciled lines.

"That's a really good picture," said Matilda when I was done. "Are you going to be an artist?"

"I might. My father's an artist."

"Is he?" asked Matilda. "I wish my father were something interesting like that. He's in public relations. Now where should we put the sign? The laundry room or the lobby? Everyone comes through the lobby. But the people who go to the laundry room read everything, because they have to wait for their laundry."

"Let's make two signs," I said.

"Yes! That's the best."

When we were finished with the two signs, Matilda put them at the head of her bed. "Well, these are some great signs," she said. "I just know they'll help us find Pink." She looked at me. "There's another thing I thought we could do."

"What?"

"Talk to people. First we could talk to Al and John and Howie. Then we'd talk to the members of the Tenants' Committee. There's one member on each floor. Then they could ask all the other people in the building about Pink."

"That sounds good." I nodded. Matilda had lots of ideas, that was for sure.

"Let's go put up our signs. We'll take the Scotch tape."

Howie was sleeping when we got to the lobby. "My mother always coughs when she sees Howie sleeping," said Matilda. She coughed.

"Uh, oh!" Howie jumped up.

"Howie, Amy's lost her white rat," said Matilda.

"A rat!"

"A white rat," I put in quickly.

"He's really pretty," said Matilda. "He's not like a real rat at all. Have you seen a white rat?"

"No white rats," said Howie. "No wild ones, either. Not here, not in the building. But they're nearby—yes, nearby." He looked quickly around the floor. "I hope your white rat didn't decide to take a walk."

"Would the wild rats hurt him?" I asked.

"Vicious, they are," said Howie. "Two big teeth in the front, like this." He held two of his fingers in front of his mouth. "They can eat through anything—wood, concrete." He put his face close to ours. "Steel!"

"They can't!" said Matilda. "Can they?"

"You better believe it," said Howie. "Downstairs . . ." He stopped as a man in a cap, carrying a package, walked up to the front door. A truck was double-parked in the street.

"Downstairs?" I asked. "Downstairs here?" But Howie was walking toward the front door, where the man in the cap was waiting. Matilda and I looked at each other.

"Maybe Pink met some wild rats," I said. "Maybe they ate him!"

"Rats don't eat rats," said Matilda. But she looked worried. "Let's put up our signs."

We put up a sign next to the mailboxes, where Matilda said everybody in the building would see it. Then we went down to the basement and put the second sign on the bulletin board in the laundry room.

"Let's talk to Al," said Matilda.

Whup! Wheeeeeeeeeeeeeee! Boom! In Al's office, Al and John were watching a rerun of "Morgan's Mercenaries."

"No rats here," said Al when we told him about Pink. "No rats of any kind."

"Don't believe what Mrs. Goldman says," said John. He looked around the floor.

"Did Mrs. Goldman see a rat?" I asked.

Rat-a-tat-tat-tat-tat-tat-tat-tat. "That Morgan, he's got a problem there," said John. Morgan was crawling on his stomach through a field as bullets struck all around him.

The phone rang on Al's desk. Al sighed and got up. "Yes, Mrs. Goldman," we heard him say. "I'll be up as soon as I have time. Maybe tomorrow."

"Men," said Morgan, "we've got to get that shoulder-mounted missile launcher. If we don't, our mission is doomed!"

Wheeeeeeeeeeee! Whup!

"Let's go," said Matilda.

"There's something about a rat—a rat and Mrs. Goldman," I said when we were outside.

"I know. They don't want to tell us. Mrs. Goldman is the head of the Tenants' Committee. Let's talk to her!"

Mrs. Goldman was in 5-H. We took the elevator upstairs. "Wait till you see Mrs. Goldman's apartment," said Matilda as we walked down the hall. "It's so *full*."

A tiny white-haired woman threw open the door of 5-H before Matilda had time to ring the bell. "Matilda! Don't tell me you're selling Girl Scout cookies again so soon!"

"No, Mrs. Goldman. This is Amy. She's staying with Ms. Farrelly in 8-J. We're looking for something Amy lost."

"Come in, come in." Mrs. Goldman had on a flowered dress, high heels, and earrings. "Sit down, sit down," she said, waving at one of the sofas. "I'll get you some cookies. Not Girl Scout cookies; I ate them." She went into the kitchen.

Mrs. Goldman's apartment was just like Liz's apartment, but it was lots more crowded. There were two sofas, lots of chairs and tables, and stands full of all kinds of things. Every wall had a bookcase. We sat on a sofa without saying anything until Mrs. Goldman came back with a tray. There were three glasses on it and a plate of cookies. "Armand's Root Beer," said Mrs. Goldman. "The best. I still buy it in Great Neck, where we lived before. And carrot cookies. Where are you from, Amy?"

"Lordsville, New Jersey."

"I was in New Jersey once," said Mrs. Goldman. "Was it in fifty-five or fifty-six? It was when we lived in Great Neck in the big house."

"Amy's lost her pet rat," said Matilda.

"Pink," I said. "He's all white except for his pink nose and feet. And the inside of his ears." All of a sudden tears started coming out of my eyes like they'd been waiting there.

Mrs. Goldman got up and brought back a little package of Kleenex. She put it in my hand.

"A pet rat?" she asked. "A *white* rat?"

I nodded, sniffing.

"That's not what I saw," said Mrs. Goldman.

"You saw a rat?" asked Matilda.

Mrs. Goldman raised a finger with a big sparkly ring. "Definitely." She lowered her voice. "I was in the laundry room yesterday, doing my sheets and towels. My cleaning woman couldn't come this week, so I had to do them myself. All of a sudden, I felt something *staring* at me." Mrs. Goldman's eyes went all around the room as if she was looking for something. "I turned slo-o-o-o-wly around and there, right in the doorway, was—a rat!"

"A white rat?" I asked.

"A gray rat," said Mrs. Goldman. "With beady eyes and ugly gray fur and a long, skinny tail. It gave me such a look. Oh, I screamed."

Matilda and I nodded, leaning forward on the sofa.

"Al came running down the hall from his office. By that time, of course, the rat was gone. Do you know what Al said?" Mrs. Goldman looked at us, her eyebrows way up on her forehead.

"What?" we asked together.

"He said it was a squirrel! Now I ask you, does a squirrel have a long, skinny tail? Does it have ugly gray fur?"

We shook our heads.

"It was a wild rat," said Mrs. Goldman. "Definitely. I'm calling a special meeting of the Tenants' Committee to discuss the maintenance of the building. My son's a lawyer, you know. Worthington, Flanigan, Lopez, Goldman, and Abeji. He's advising me. Have some more carrot cookies."

I looked at Matilda. "There *is* a wild rat in the building! What if Pink meets it?"

"Pink probably didn't go to the basement," said Matilda quickly. "He probably went somewhere where there's food. Like another apartment. We'll keep looking for him." She stood up. "Thanks for the cookies and root beer, Mrs. Goldman. We have to go."

By lunchtime, we had talked to all of the members of the Tenants' Committee who were home. None of them had seen any rats, white or gray. The last person we talked to lived in a penthouse on the top floor. "Tom Tyrell," said Matilda as we rode up on the elevator. "He's an actor. He used to be on Broadway, my mother says. That's when he got the penthouse. Now he's in the soaps sometimes."

There were only four apartments on the top floor and they had letters instead of numbers. Matilda pressed the bell of B. Nothing happened. She pressed the bell again. We heard these slow footsteps coming toward the door. All of a sudden it flew open.

"Matilda!" The tall old man who opened the door was wearing sandals and shorts. He had lots of gray hair. "I was reading on my terrace," he said in a loud voice. "Join me, join me."

We followed him through a room with lots of windows and out a glass door. It was a garden! There were pink flowers and blue flowers and red flowers and yellow flowers. There was a tree, too. Underneath the tree were some chairs.

We sat down in the chairs. "Your garden is nice this year," said Matilda.

"It's the new fertilizer," said Tom Tyrell. "City-Life, it's called. Makes anything grow. And who is this young lady?"

"Amy Schultz," said Matilda. "She's staying with Ms. Farrelly in 8-J."

"Ah—the lovely Elizabeth," said Tom Tyrell, throwing out his arms. "She makes me feel young." His voice went rumble, rumble, all around the terrace as if he had a microphone. A pigeon sitting on the wall got up and flew away. "And where are you from, Amy?" he asked, looking at me.

"New Jersey."

"New Jersey! A magnificent state! From its white beaches to its forested hills! From its cranberry bogs to its rushing rivers! Oh, I know New Jersey well. I've played in theaters all over the state."

"Gosh," I said. "You're the only person I've met here who knows anything about New Jersey."

"Amy's lost her white rat," said Matilda.

"A white rat! A most intelligent creature, the rat. I had one as a boy. Took it with me when we opened in *Whoopee* in Pittsburgh. It disappeared there."

"Did you ever find it?" I asked.

"Never—we had to return to New York. But no doubt your rat is somewhere in the building, Amy. I shall keep an eye out for it."

"Thanks," I said. "Are you really in the soaps?"

"Occasionally. My last role was as the butler in 'Scottsdale.' He was killed by a burglar, unfortunately." He sighed. "Since then I haven't worked much. I live mostly on unemployment. But Mrs. Goldman tells me the building can't raise the rent on my penthouse because of my age. It's the law!"

"Her son's a lawyer," said Matilda.

"Worthington, Flanigan, Lopez, Goldman, and Abeji," said Mr. Tyrell, nodding.

"I'm learning classic tap this summer, Mr. Tyrell," said Matilda.

"Classic tap! I was a chorus boy in musicals when I started out." Tom Tyrell got to his feet and shuffled back and forth in his sandals, humming. "What's this?" he asked.

"Shuffle off to Buffalo," shouted Matilda. "Oh, I love that. "It's Ruby Keeler's big number in *Forty-Second Street*. But we haven't learned it yet."

"Just follow me," said Tom Tyrell, taking Matilda's arm. "It's kick, cross, other leg, kick, cross, other leg, and turrrrn!"

Matilda danced beside him. They sang something that sounded like "Off we gotta shuffle, shuffle off to Buff-a-lo-o." What a weird song! But it looked like such fun to tap-dance.

When we were leaving, Tom Tyrell said, "You know, Amy, you look like Ruby Keeler. I knew her when she was on Broadway. She was a pretty one!"

63

"He said it, too," I said to Matilda when we were back in the hall. "About Ruby Keeler, I mean."

"You do, really."

I was pretty, I thought! "This winter, I'm going to learn to tap-dance," I said. Because suddenly I could see myself tap-dancing, wearing a hat like the one Ruby Keeler wore in the picture in Matilda's bedroom. "Isn't she talented!" people would say. And other people would say, "Isn't she pretty!"

"If you come next summer, you can sign up for Classic Tap!" said Matilda. "I'll be taking Classic Tap II and we can dance together!"

"Yeah!"

I forgot all about Pink while we were talking about tap dancing, but when I got to the door of apartment 8-J, I remembered. Pink was gone. Maybe Pink was dead. As soon as I opened the door, Liz looked up from her computer.

"Your father would like you to call him, Amy."

I dialed the number. "It's me."

"Tulip, Liz called me about Pink today. I'm very, very sorry. I like Pink."

I wanted to tell him how it was all Liz's fault but I couldn't because Liz was sitting right there at her computer. And even though she was typing, I knew she was listening.

"You might find Pink," said my father, "but Liz

and I would like to buy you another white rat right now."

"No! I don't want another one. I want Pink!"

"I know, Tulip. Pink is special. But don't be too hard on Liz, will you? She feels bad. I'll see you this weekend."

I hung up the phone. I couldn't tell my father on the phone, but if it hadn't been for Liz dropping the cage, Pink wouldn't be dead. It was all her fault, and I was glad she felt bad.

Chapter Six

◆

I didn't talk to Liz all week. Well, only when I had to, like when she asked me a question. It was very quiet in the apartment when the two of us were there together. After a while I wished I could talk to Liz, but I kept telling myself that it was her fault that Pink was dead.

When I got up on Friday, Liz had on a suit instead of her jeans. "I'm going to have lunch with an editor," she said. "When I get back, Amy, we've got to *talk*. Lunch is in the refrigerator."

I didn't say anything, of course. Liz walked out the door carrying her briefcase.

Maybe, I thought, I could stay in Matilda's apartment until my mother came home. I would ask her, I would ask her today! But then I remembered that Matilda was going to the museums again with the Museum Mavens, these girls from her school.

I went over to Liz's desk and got a piece of her paper and an envelope and a pen. "Dear Mother," I wrote. "Pink is lost. Liz was dusting his cage and she dropped it. Maybe Maud the dog ate Pink. Maud is a mean dog. Or else Maud scared him so he ran away. There is a reward for Pink but I don't think anybody will find him. I think Pink is dead."

I stopped because I was crying. After a while, I wrote: "I met a girl in the apartment building. Her name is Matilda. I like her. She tap-dances." I stopped again. Should I say something about my father? No, it would just make my mother mad. "Write as soon as you can," I finished. "I love you. Amy."

After I licked the envelope and closed it up, I remembered something. I opened it up. "Can I take tap dancing lessons in Lordsville?" I wrote.

The envelope would need more stamps than a regular envelope, I knew, so I'd have to give it to Liz to take to the post office. I put the letter next to Pink's empty cage. Pink! I turned the little wheel inside the cage with my finger.

The morning lasted a long time. I walked Maud and talked to Howie and looked at a soap and drew a picture of the pigeon. This picture was better than the first one. I hadn't noticed before, but pigeons have orange eyes.

I went into the kitchen. The lunch was in the refrigerator with a little sign in front of it that said Amy's Lunch. There was a chicken salad sandwich, a bowl of homemade chicken soup from this big kettle of soup Liz had made, and a high-fiber muffin.

A pan on the stove had a sign in front of it that said Pan for Soup. Liz was always making these signs. While the soup was heating, I opened up the sandwich and took all the celery out of the chicken salad. I hate celery.

I put the lunch on the table. The soup was good and the high-fiber muffin was good, too. Maud the dog put her paw on my knee when I was eating the muffin. She loves muffins.

Of course I wasn't speaking to Maud, either, except to say bad things to her. "Murderer!" I said.

Maud the dog whined and lay down under Liz's desk.

After lunch, I copied my pigeon drawing on a good sheet of paper. By then I was tired of sitting. I wished I could tap-dance. Then I could practice and get really good. People would say, "Doesn't she look like Ruby Keeler?"

I got up and went into the living room, where there was more room. I moved my feet the way Matilda had shown me. I didn't have tap shoes, of course, but I stamped my feet real hard instead.

Stamp, stamp, stamp, turn.

Sideways, sideways, turn.

Back and forth, back and forth.

This was fun!

Stampety, stampety, stamp! Stampety, stampety, stamp!

Sl-i-i-i-i-i-i-de.

I went faster.

STAMP, STAMP, STAMP . . .

All the little things in the apartment were jiggling back and forth as if they were dancing, too. I giggled. They were dancing along with me! Maud began to bark.

STAMPETY, STAMPETY, STAMP!

Yap! Yap! Yap!

Crash!

I stopped dancing. Maud the statue was on the floor, broken in millions of pieces.

Yap! Yap! Yap!

"Shut up, dumb dog!" I cried.

The statue was in too many pieces to be put back together, that was for sure. Liz liked this statue a lot. She'd be mad. Maybe she'd get that look with the hard, shiny eyes and yell, like my father. I hate it when people get like that.

I got the broom from the hall closet and swept up all the pieces of Maud the statue into a pile on a piece of the *New York Times.* I picked the newspaper up by the corners and put it on the table. Then I went into the bedroom and sat down in front of the black-and-white TV and turned on a game show. I didn't like game shows, but I didn't want to think about the statue. I watched TV until I heard Liz opening the front door.

Yap! Yap! Yap! Maud was dancing all around Liz when I went out into the hall. "What a lunch," said Liz. "I'm half asleep. But I think I sold a book. What's this?" She was looking at the pieces of Maud the statue.

"I broke it, I'm very sorry, I don't think it's going to go back together," I said very fast.

"Maud," whispered Liz. She picked up one of the pieces from the newspaper and looked at it in her hand. "I bought it in England," she said. "It reminded me of—the poem." She sniffed.

This was even worse than yelling. Grown-ups shouldn't cry. It makes them look like kids. When grown-ups cry I want to run away. I looked at the floor. Oh, I wished I were somewhere else! Maybe I could stay with my awful cousin Jessica after all, maybe. . . .

"What were you doing when it broke?" asked

Liz, wiping her eyes with one hand. She took a big envelope out of her desk and poured the pieces of Maud the statue into it.

"Dancing. Tap-dancing. Everything started jiggling. I didn't mean to break it."

"Tap-dancing! Tap-dancing! Ohhhhhh!" Liz put the big envelope on her desk and ran into the bedroom. The door banged behind her. But I could hear her crying. This was awful! Why did my mother have to go so far away and leave me here with a grown-up who cried? I looked out the window. There was a pigeon on the sill again. It looked at me.

"I wish I was a pigeon," I said. Pigeons didn't have to worry about statues and things like that. Pigeons never cried or yelled. Pigeon mothers never went to places like Africa. Being a pigeon would be a nice life.

Maud the dog whined and tried to put her paw on my knee. "Leave me alone!" I said.

The bedroom door opened and Liz came out in her shirt and jeans. Her eyes were red but she wasn't crying any more. "Amy," said Liz, "let's talk."

We went into the living room and sat on the sofa, side by side. The pigeon was still on the window sill. It looked at us. "You didn't mean to break Maud," said Liz.

"I didn't!" I said, shaking my head.

"And I didn't mean to let Pink go. And Maud didn't mean to scare him."

"Losing Pink is lots worse than breaking Maud the statue! Because Pink was alive!"

Liz drew in her breath. "That's right. It *is* worse." She touched my hand with the tips of her long fingers. "Friends?"

I pulled my hand away. "You clean too much. If you hadn't been cleaning, Pink would be here, alive!"

"Oh, Amy." She looked into my face. "It was an *accident*. And people have different standards about cleaning. I like things more organized than your mother does. It's just my way."

"Anyway," I said, "you never look at me all day. You just stare at the computer like, like a zombie!"

"Do I?" asked Liz.

I nodded.

Liz gave this big, big sigh and looked at her lap. "Well, I guess I do. I'm not used to having a child around. I'm not used to having *anyone* around." She gave me this sad look. "And I'm in a bad place with my novel."

We both sat and looked out the window. The pigeon took off, its wings flapping. Liz turned to me and took my hand in both of hers. "I promise to look at you occasionally during the day! How's that?" She smiled this tiny, tiny smile.

"Well, it would be *better*," I said. Liz's hands

were warm, like my mother's and my father's. I wondered if everybody's hands were warm like that.

"Friends?" said Liz again.

"Friends," I agreed.

"Will you pet Maud?"

Maud whined and put her paw on my knee again.

I shook the paw. It was warm, too. Maud licked my hand.

"But no dancing in the living room, okay?

"Okay!" I felt happy all of a sudden. Being mad at people is very hard.

"Do you remember your father's coming for dinner tomorrow?" asked Liz. "What'll I make?"

"Pizza!"

"Pizza? Well, I do have a recipe."

"Let's order pizza from the pizza store."

"No, Amy, your father is a guest. I want to make something for him myself." Liz went into the kitchen and came out with a book. "Here it is. Um-hmm. I have everything but the cheese and green pepper. I'll get that tomorrow and some salad greens. And a bottle of wine. And some Italian ice cream."

She hummed to herself as she wrote all this down on a piece of paper. She was always writing lists of things.

I never heard of a homemade pizza. I wished we

could get some from the store. That's what my mother does when Brad comes.

We had dinner at McFry's. Coming back, I saw Matilda going into the apartment house.

"Matilda!"

Matilda turned around and waved. Liz went up in the elevator while Matilda and I sat on the stone wall next to the front door.

"Something's happened," I told her. I told her about breaking Maud the statue.

"My mother won't let me dance in the apartment," said Matilda. "It makes things shake. And the neighbors complain."

A pigeon walked right in front of us and a little feather fell off it. The feather drifted down to the sidewalk. I picked up the feather. I wondered if this pigeon was the same one outside our window. "We're sort of friends, now, Liz and me," I said. "Because she didn't mean to let Pink go. And I didn't mean to break the statue. And I'm talking to Maud the dog, too."

"It's hard being mad at someone for a long time," said Matilda. "Especially when they're always around."

Matilda understood! "It is!" I said. "I felt awful!"

"Anyway, Ms. Farrelly is kind of nice, I think," said Matilda. "For a grown-up, I mean. You can't really be friends with them. Not like us."

"I know," I said. We smiled at each other.

"Come down and watch TV with me and my mother tomorrow night," said Matilda. "There's a special program on 'Great Theater.' "

"My father is coming to dinner tomorrow night," I said. I felt proud. My father was coming to dinner to see me!

When I got back to the apartment Liz was reading a book. She read books all the time when she wasn't working.

As I walked through the hall, Liz said, "Amy, would you make your bed after you get up?"

"Mother never makes the beds," I said.

"Well you know the old saying, 'When in Rome . . .' " said Liz.

"I don't know it."

" 'When in Rome, do as the Romans do,' " said Liz. "It would really be nice if you'd make the bed every day." I went in the bedroom and closed the door. I was friends with Liz but not *good* friends. Because Liz really did have a lot of weird ideas. What was the use of making the bed every day if you were just going to mess it up every night?

I put the pigeon feather next to Pink's cage on the chest of drawers. I opened the little door and spun the little wheel with my hand. "Oh, Pink," I said.

Saturday morning, when I got up, Liz was already cleaning. And on Saturday afternoon, she spent a long time making the pizza. It looked funny when she was finished, not like a store pizza. She made little cakes she called petty fours, too. She put flowers in a vase in the living room. Then she put on this pair of long, black pants and a shiny shirt and a silver necklace. Her hair is very long and black and curly. She looked almost as pretty as my mother.

I waited for my father in front of the apartment house. He was taking the subway uptown. I saw him as soon as he turned the corner and I ran all the way down the street to meet him.

"Hello, Tulip," he said, looking at me like he hadn't seen me for a long time. He was carrying two packages.

"What are those?" I asked.

He handed me the big lumpy one and I tore it open right there. "Oh," I said. It was Janine's yellow poncho.

"Janine found it under the sofa," he said. "You don't have to wear it." He smiled at me.

He took my hand and we walked down the sidewalk together. "How are you and the Godmother making out?" he asked.

"We're friends now. She's sorry about Pink. And I'm sorry about the statue." I told him about breaking Maud the statue.

"It's too bad about Maud the statue. But I'm glad you and Liz are friends," said my father, squeezing my hand. "Tell me about the tap dancing."

The first thing my father did when he got to Liz's apartment was give Liz the other package. She opened it. It was a little painting of a purple tree.

"Oh, Carl!"

My father looked all around, the way he always does when he goes someplace new.

"Who's this?" He pointed at the bust of Alfred, Lord Tennyson. He read the letters on the bust. "Ah!" Standing in the middle of the living room floor, he said:

> *"My heart would hear her and beat,*
> *Were it earth in an earthly bed;*
> *My dust would hear her and beat,*
> *Had I lain for a century dead."*

"Oh, Carl! You know Tennyson!"

"He wrote some good lines."

I was still holding the yellow poncho. "What's that, Amy?" asked Liz.

I held it up.

"Oh!" said Liz. "How . . . unusual."

"A present to Amy from a friend of mine, Janine," said my father. "I don't think Amy likes it much."

"It really isn't her color," said Liz.

Liz and I smiled at each other. Then I took the poncho to the bedroom and put it in the back of the closet. When I got back, my father and Liz were looking at the stuffed bird on top of the cupboard. My father liked all the funny things Liz had.

He liked the dinner, too. "Do you eat like this all the time, Amy?" he asked when we were eating dessert.

"Yes." I took another little cake. Liz told me they're spelled p-e-t-i-t f-o-u-r-s. They were very good.

After dinner, my father told us about some of the artists in his building. One was Mr. Mess, only that wasn't his real name. Mr. Mess put things like real food and toothpaste on his paintings.

"If you brush up against one of those things, watch out!" my father said. "In Mess's last show, the youngest Mess ate a whole painting."

I put another petit four in my mouth, a pink one. Liz laughed at almost everything my father said. After a while, she showed him her computer files.

"Beautiful and organized," said my father, smiling at Liz and looking at her instead of the computer files.

"If you're organized you can get more done, Carl. You can put all your contacts on the computer, for instance."

I yawned. It was boring sitting there listening to them talk about the computer. I got up and stood next to the computer. "Can you take me to the aquarium?" I asked my father.

"I haven't seen the dolphins in a while," said my father. "I wonder what they're up to? Yes, let's go! And maybe Liz would like to go, too."

Liz smiled. "I'm a dolphin lover myself."

"Let's pick a weekday," said my father. "The dolphins have lots of people over on weekends."

Liz looked at her calendar—it was on the computer, too—and so we were all going to the aquarium on Wednesday. I was disappointed. I wanted to go to the aquarium with my father, just the two of us.

The next morning, the first thing Liz said to me was, "Who is Janine, Amy?"

"She's this friend of my father's. She lives in the same building. She weaves these awful things."

"Like the yellow cape?"

"It's something the Fumalee Indians wear when it rains."

"Are your father and Janine . . . good friends?"

I thought about it. "Well, I think so. She's always poking him, you know?"

"I wonder how old she is."

"I don't know."

"Younger than me?"

"Yes." I was sure about that.

Liz sighed. "Do you know how old I am, Amy?"

"As old as my mother."

"Six months older. I'm thirty-three."

Liz walked around the living room with the little purple tree painting, holding it up against the wall in different places.

"What about here?" she asked.

"It looks nice there."

She got a hammer and a nail and hung it up. My father's painting did look nice hanging on Liz's wall.

Liz stood back and looked at the purple tree. "It's too bad your father has so much trouble selling his work," she said. "He's so talented, but I'm afraid he's a little disorganized. I mean, he doesn't keep track of his work. He doesn't make contacts."

"He can't ever find anything," I said. "Once he lost his car for two weeks."

"Where was it?"

"In a parking lot."

Liz smiled as she used this tiny little brush to brush up some crumbs I couldn't even see on the table. "Sometimes a very talented person isn't good at dealing with real life. They need someone to help them."

It was right then I got this fabulous idea, one of the best ideas I'd ever had. Liz and my father! She could look after the real life part while he painted. She would keep track of his work! She would make contacts! Then he'd sell his paintings and give money to my mother! He would get a bigger apartment, too, an apartment Liz would keep clean.

There would be lots of room for me!

And with Liz around, my father wouldn't have any time for Janine.

I could tell Liz and my father liked each other. Maybe I could sort of—help it along. Yes! I would ask him to take me places he could take Liz, too, like the aquarium. I had to talk about this with Matilda right away! Then I remembered. Today Matilda was visiting her father, and tomorrow morning she took her tap lesson. I would have to wait until Monday afternoon.

"Have you made your bed?" asked Liz as I sat in my room, looking at the black-and-white TV.

Of course, I thought, as I straightened the sheets, there would be problems having Liz around, too.

Chapter Seven

◆

I've got lots to tell you!" I said when Matilda opened the door.

We went into her bedroom and sat on the bed. "Liz and my father like each other," I said. "And I've got this great idea!"

"What?" asked Matilda, her brown eyes very big.

I took a deep breath. "My father and Liz could get married, and then Liz could take care of all the real-life things for him! She could clean up his apartment and make contacts for him and keep his files! See, she's organized and he's, he's . . ."

"Disorganized?" asked Matilda.

"Yes!" I cried. "And if Liz got him organized, he could sell his paintings. He could give my mother money. And he'd have room for me!"

But Matilda didn't look like she thought this was a great idea. "Don't you care?" she asked. "Don't you care that he'd be marrying someone else, someone who's not your mother?"

"I'd like him to marry my mother again but he won't and she won't. Because every time they get together they fight."

I remembered the last time they had been together, in a McFry's with me. They said mean things to each other all the time we were eating. My father's eyes were hard and shiny and he talked in a loud voice. People looked at us. And then I threw up in the ladies' room. Afterward my mother said it was all my father's fault. And when I saw my father he said it was all my mother's fault.

"They don't like each other any more," I said. "It's awful when they get together."

"My mother says people who get divorced never, never, never get married to each other again," said Matilda, shaking her long black hair every time she said "never."

"And Liz would be lots better than Janine," I said. "With Janine, there would be the two giant

83

looms. There would never be any room for me, ever."

Matilda was nodding her head slowly now. "And you'd have to wear those awful woven things," she said. "Maybe it *would* be a good idea if your father married Liz. And you know what? They could live in her apartment! And you could visit them all summer!"

"No, it's too small," I said. "My father does these big, big paintings of trees."

"Then they could live in his apartment."

"That's too small, too. But they could get a bigger apartment in my father's building because then they'd be a family. Families get bigger apartments. And they'd have room for me to stay all summer!"

"You could take Classic Tap I while I take Classic Tap II! And you could join the Museum Mavens!"

"Yes! I'm going to try to sort of help things along. Like asking him to take me places he can take Liz, too. Saturday night, I asked him to take me to the aquarium and now he's taking us both, me and Liz."

"It's working already!" cried Matilda.

"Yes!"

Matilda and I hugged each other. It would be so great to see her all summer. Because now Matilda was my best friend.

Matilda looked at her pig watch. "It's almost three o'clock!"

We ran down the basement steps. When we got to the door of Al's office, we heard Paverly Yard's voice.

"Eric, I'm your wife. Don't you remember me? Don't you remember our apartment? Our wedding day? Our dog?"

"Yap, yap, yap!"

"The dog remembers him," said John. "Dogs have good memories. Hello, girls."

"I don't remember anything!" cried Eric. His face filled the whole screen. He's very handsome.

Paverly Yard began to cry.

"It's so sad," said Matilda.

Gillian, the person Paverly Yard plays, is a nurse, so she knows all these doctors. Next we saw her in the office of Dr. Walter Emory, a world-famous specialist in what Eric had. "We'll do everything we can, Gillian," said Dr. Emory. He grabbed Paverly Yard's hand and squeezed it.

"Uh-oh," said John, shaking his head.

"I'm sure Dr. Emory can cure Eric," I said.

"But, Amy," said Matilda, "he's in love with Gillian, remember? He doesn't want to cure Eric."

Paverly Yard's face filled the whole screen. "I know I can depend on you, Walter," she said.

Dr. Emory's face filled the whole screen as Paverly Yard left the office. He had a funny look on his face.

When "Los Angeles Emergency" was over, John said, "Anybody seen your rat, Amy?" He looked all around the floor.

"Nobody," I said. Al was looking at the floor, too.

Matilda and I stood in front of the elevators for a long time, waiting for one to come. "Al and John looked at the floor again when John asked about Pink," I said.

"I know," said Matilda, looking at the floor herself. "I wonder how big they are."

"Bigger than Pink," I said, my eyes filling with tears.

"Oh, Amy, I'm *sure* Pink's not down here," said Matilda. "Would you go down here, if you were a rat?"

"No," I had to agree. But why hadn't anybody called 8-J if he'd gone somewhere else?

The elevator finally came. *Clank, clank, clank. Crash!*

"The elevator really sounds awful today," said Matilda. "I have to return a book to the library. Can you come with me?"

"Where is it? Liz doesn't want me to go off the block, unless I go to the supermarket or drugstore across the street."

"It's four blocks away but it's really safe. Liz goes there. We'll call and ask her."

We called Liz when we got to Matilda's apartment and she said it was okay for me to go to the library. Matilda got her book, and we went out and stood in front of the elevators again. This time the elevator came right away.

Clank, clank, clank. Crash! Boom! Eeeeeeeeeeeeooooooohhhh. The elevator door opened with this awful moan. "Why don't you get a book from the library?" asked Matilda as we were going down. "You can take one out on my card."

"No, I don't want to."

"This is the third time I've read this book," said Matilda, looking at the book in her hand. "It's my favorite."

Whump! The elevator stopped but the doors didn't open. Matilda pressed the button for the first floor again. Nothing happened. She pressed it again. Nothing.

"It's stuck!" cried Matilda.

She pressed another button, a red one that read Alarm.

There was a sound like a loud doorbell.

"That's the alarm," said Matilda. "Now Al will come."

"How long will we be here?" I asked.

"Last winter, someone was in here two hours," said Matilda.

"Two hours!"

We heard the sound of footsteps far away. They

went slowly up the stairs. The footsteps got closer and closer.

"Who's in there?" shouted Al's voice.

"Me, Al—and Amy!"

"Press 'Penthouse'!" said Al.

Matilda pressed the button that said *P*.

Nothing happened.

"I did, Al!" yelled Matilda.

"Try 'Basement.' "

Matilda pressed the button that said *B*.

Nothing happened.

"Did you press it?" called Al.

"Yes!"

"It's stuck," said Al. "I'll call the repairman. Just sit tight, girls, don't worry."

The footsteps went down the stairs.

My stomach felt funny. What if we didn't get out for two hours? What if we didn't get out for three hours? The elevator was so small! There wasn't anything to do. There wasn't anyplace to go!

"Do you have to go to the bathroom?" asked Matilda.

I hadn't thought about that. "No—not yet."

"Me, either," said Matilda. "Oh, we're so lucky, Amy!"

"Lucky! Lucky to be stuck in this tiny little elevator?" I put my hand on my stomach. Maybe I was going to throw up.

Matilda waved her book. "Lucky because [I] got my favorite book with me! I'll read it to y[ou] while we wait!"

Matilda slid down the wall until she was sittin[g] on the floor. I did the same thing. There wasn'[t] anything else to do. What if we were on here four hours? Or longer? If I ever got off, I would never take the elevator again, never!

Matilda opened her book. She cleared her throat.

" 'When Mary Lennox was sent to Misselthwaite Manor to live with her uncle, everybody said she was the most disagreeable-looking child ever seen.' "

It sounded boring, like the books I'd read for school. Well, I would just try to think about something else. I closed my eyes. I wondered what my mother was doing. I wondered what Pink was doing. If he was alive, that is.

Matilda turned a page. " 'There's near a hundred rooms in it, though most of them's shut up and locked . . . a big porch round it and gardens and trees with branches trailing to the ground.' "

A hundred rooms! What a big house. And all those gardens. I decided I might as well listen after all. Matilda's voice went on and on. After a while, it was like I wasn't in the elevator at all. I was in this big old house with walled gardens in back of it, and somewhere in the middle of the gardens was

another garden, a garden without a door. It made me shiver to think about it, but it was a good kind of shivering.

"Girls!" It was Al's voice again. We hadn't even heard his footsteps. "The repairman is on the way. Your mother is here, Matilda. And Miss Farrelly."

"Are you all right, Matilda?" came the voice of Amy's mother.

"Yes, Mom. We've got a book. We're reading."

"Oh, that's good. The repairman is on the way."

"Amy!" This time it was Liz's voice. "I knew this would happen! Thank goodness you have a book. The repairman is on the way."

"We know!" I called back. "Go on," I said to Matilda.

After Matilda started again, I was outside the big house, holding the key. . . .

" 'She was standing inside the secret garden,' " read Matilda. She stopped reading to look at me. "I *love* this part!"

"Oh, go on!"

"Girls!" It was Al's voice again. "It's going to be a little while because the regular repairman, his uncle died. So the other repairman is taking all the emergency calls."

We could hear the voices of Liz and Mrs. Matthews talking to Al. They sounded mad. There was another voice, too.

"Worthington, Flanigan, Lopez, Goldman, and Abeji," the voice was saying.

"Mrs. Goldman," said Matilda.

"The service in this building is going downhill!" Mrs. Goldman's voice said. "Definitely! The Tenants' Committee will hold a special meeting on this."

"Amy, Matilda!" It was Liz again. "You'll have to wait a while longer.

"We know, Ms. Farrelly," said Matilda. "It's okay. This is a really long book."

"I like it," I called to Liz.

"We'll all go to McFry's when you get out," promised Liz.

Matilda began to read again. Soon I was walking down a dark hall toward the sound of someone crying. Oh, who could it be?

"He's here!" It was Al's voice.

"He's here, girls!" said Mrs. Matthews.

"Amy, Matilda, the repairman is here!" said Liz.

"It's about time!" said Mrs. Goldman.

Bang! Clang! The repairman was doing something in the basement. Suddenly we began to move.

"Yay!" cried Matilda. She looked at her pig watch. "We were stuck three hours!"

"What happens?" I asked. "What happens in the room? You've got to tell me!"

The elevator stopped but this time the door opened right away. We were on the first floor. Howie was standing there, looking worried. "Girls!" he cried. He grabbed both of us together in a big hug.

Then the stairway door flew open and Mrs. Matthews and Liz came rushing through it. Liz hugged me. Mrs. Matthews hugged Matilda. Then Mrs. Matthews hugged me and Liz hugged Matilda.

Mrs. Goldman came through the stairway door in her high heels and another pretty dress. She hugged us, too.

"We were in there three hours!" said Matilda. "That's a new record!"

"Definitely!" said Mrs. Goldman. "The maintenance in this building is going downhill!" She looked at Howie. "And some of the services, too!"

Howie walked away and looked out the front door.

I grabbed Matilda's arm. "Matilda! What happens next in the book? You have to tell me!"

"I'll let you keep the book tonight," said Matilda. "And tomorrow, we'll go to the library and I'll take it out again. Then you can read the whole thing if you want to."

She handed me the book.

I held it carefully. "This is a *good* book," I said.

"Who's for McFry's?" Liz was saying. "I'm hungry enough for the Tyrannosaurus."

That's the giant burger with six-inch fries that look like teeth. McFry's was six blocks down the avenue, so we started walking to the corner, even Mrs. Goldman. Matilda and I walked together, behind the grown-ups. I could hear Mrs. Goldman's voice.

". . . And Howie sleeping all the time," she was saying. "Why, anybody could walk by that man!"

". . . Physical condition?" came Liz's voice. ". . . Talking to Howie last week when he was sitting down and he fell asleep! I heard about some medicine you can take for . . ."

Matilda and I walked slow so we got further behind them. We were going by the metal gate that leads to the basement of the building when I saw it. It looked like a cat, a little cat, and it ran across the sidewalk in front of Matilda and me.

"A little cat, Matilda!" I said, pointing at the gate.

Matilda stopped and grabbed my arm. "That's not a cat," she whispered.

The animal started to go into a hole right next to the gate, but then it turned around for a second. It was the size of a little cat but lower, and it had funny gray fur and a long skinny tail without any fur. Its eyes looked right at me. They were like two black beads!

"It's a rat!" I whispered back to Matilda. "A wild rat!"

The rat disappeared into the hole. I knew where the hole led. Right into the basement!

"There *are* wild rats in the basement, there are!" I said.

"Are you coming, girls?" called Mrs. Matthews. The grown-ups were at the corner already.

Matilda grabbed my hand. "Come on." We started to run. "Don't tell Mrs. Goldman," said Matilda. "She'll make a big fuss."

We ran down the sidewalk to the corner. "Matilda, I know the wild rats ate Pink," I whispered as we walked down the avenue. "They're much bigger than he is! That's why nobody in the building has seen Pink! He's dead!"

Chapter Eight

◆

I wish I could have a dolphin," I said.

We were on the subway coming back from the aquarium, and my father and Liz had started talking about his career. Up to then, we'd been having fun. Then Liz said he should try sending out postcards with a photograph of his painting that won the prize last year. And he said it was too expensive. And she said it was worth it.

"I wish I could have a dolphin, a baby dolphin," I said. At the aquarium, one of the dolphins had this cute baby dolphin. It looked like a dolphin doll.

"Nobody but Doris Duke can afford a dolphin," said my father. This was a joke. There's this very rich woman, Doris Duke, who lives near Lordsville, and when my father lived with us he used to say only Doris Duke could afford things.

"Amy, would you like to have a gerbil?" asked Liz. "I saw one at Fur and Fin and they're so cute!"

"No!" I said. "I'm waiting. I'm waiting until I know for *sure* about Pink." That made me think about the rat I saw the day we got stuck on the elevator. I hadn't seen another one, even though I had looked all over the basement.

"This is it," said Liz, getting up.

We got off the subway and climbed up the steps.

"Carl, come up to the apartment and I'll show you this postcard I got last week from Wanda Bottemly," said Liz. "She won . . ."

"Wanda Bottemly!" interrupted my father, and then he said a bad word and his eyes got hard and shiny the way they do when he's mad.

But Liz smiled. "Well, she isn't the greatest artist, but she does know how to market herself, Carl." She took his hand. "Come up."

And my father smiled. He didn't look mad anymore.

"Yes, come up!" I said, pulling on his other hand.

"Please, ladies. Restrain yourselves. I'll come up!"

Howie was sleeping when we went by him. I thought Liz would go to get her mail, like she always does in the afternoon, but she just pressed the elevator button. The elevator door opened right away.

"Aren't you going to get the mail?" I asked.

"Why don't you get it, Amy," said Liz. "Here, I'll give you the key." She gave me the little key, and as the door closed, I could see her and my father smiling at each other.

Usually Liz couldn't wait to get the mail. She knew just when it came and she went down on the elevator and picked it up. But she didn't open anything until she got upstairs. She had this special letter opener that made a little slit in the tops of the envelopes. Then she took the letters out and read them.

Liz's box was so high up I had to stand on tiptoe to reach it. It was all full of mail. Liz got more mail than anyone I ever knew. Matilda said all writers get lots of mail.

I looked through the mail. Lots of envelopes with Liz's name on them, a magazine, and a blue envelope with a funny stamp. The blue envelope had my name on it! I turned the envelope so I could read the name on the stamp. "Republic of Wambia," it said.

"It's a letter for me from my mother!" I cried.

Howie sat up straight on the sofa and looked all around.

"From Wambia! That's in Africa!"

"Africa!" said Howie.

I sat down next to Howie and tore open the envelope. She hadn't gotten my letter yet, I could tell. ". . . Writing from the capital before I go into the bush . . . rat stew . . . very humid . . . met the most interesting man . . . new folktale just for you . . . I love you and don't forget it."

The folktale was on two extra pages. At the top it said, "The Eagle's Child." I folded the letter slowly and put it and the folktale carefully back inside the blue envelope. I would read the folktale upstairs. I could hear my mother's voice as if she were standing right in front of me. "I love you and don't forget it," she said.

"What kind of place is that, Africa?" asked Howie.

"It's hot. They eat rat stew."

"Rat stew! Now that's something I wouldn't want to eat."

I thought about the wild rat I had seen outside the basement gate. "These rats are different from the rats around here, my mother says. They taste good. People like to eat them."

"I'll eat most anything!" said Howie. "Lamb. Liver. I ate smoked eel once at a wedding. But not rat. Have you heard anything about your white rat?"

"No," I said. "Howie, on Monday we saw . . ."

But just then a man came up to the door with a package and Howie got up. I went over to the elevator and pushed the button. When I got to 8-J, Liz and my father were sitting close together on the sofa. I put Liz's mail on her desk and stood in front of the sofa. Maud the dog came over and put her paw on my leg. I leaned down to pet her.

"I got a letter from Mother!" I said.

"Oh, how nice," said Liz, with a quick look at my father. "Is she out in the bush yet?"

"No, she's still in the capital. She ate rat stew! She says it's good."

"She's so adventurous," said Liz, looking at my father out of the corner of her eyes. "When we were in college, she was always the one who wanted to *do* things, go places. . . . I was the scaredy-cat."

"Were you?" I asked. This was interesting.

My father put his hand on Liz's hand. "I like scaredy-cats." he said.

Liz and my father stared at each other, smiling, just the way they had on the elevator. It was like they'd forgotten all about me. And my mother.

"She sent a folktale, a folktale just for me," I said.

"Oh, Amy, can I read it later?" asked Liz.

"Maybe," I said.

My father took my hand. He squeezed it and smiled.

"I'm going to read it myself right now," I said. "Come on, Maud!"

Maud and I went into the bedroom. I sat on the bed and opened the envelope. Maud sat next to the bed and looked up at me.

"This folktale is called 'The Eagle's Child,' " I said, unfolding the two sheets of paper.

Maud wagged her tail.

"Once Eagle laid her egg in a nest of sticks on a big rock. A river flowed beside the rock. Then the hungry time before the harvest came. Eagle had no food.

" 'I must fly to another place to find food,' Eagle said to herself. 'But who will watch my egg?'

"Eagle's good friend was a lizard. 'Lizard, my friend,' said Eagle, 'I must look for food far away. Will you watch my egg?'

" 'Of course,' said Lizard.

"Eagle flew away and Lizard lay next to the eagle egg.

"After a few days, the egg hatched and a baby eagle climbed out. 'Mother, mother!' it cried.

" 'Shhhhhhhh!' warned Lizard.

"It was too late. In the forest, where all crocodiles used to live, Crocodile heard the baby eagle's cry. He crawled to the bottom of the big rock and looked up.

"When Lizard saw Crocodile, she ran to the top of the tallest tree and sang a song.

" *'Eagle, Eagle, please come!*
A crocodile has heard your child.
Linkpin, a linkpin, lakpan.'

"Eagle was so far away she couldn't understand what the song said. The big bird flew partway home and sat in a tree in Kolahun to listen.

"Crocodile crawled slowly up the big rock.

"Lizard sang again, louder.

" *'Eagle, Eagle, please come!*
A crocodile is near your child.
Linkpin, a linkpin, lakpan.'

"Eagle still couldn't understand what the song said. So she flew farther and sat in a tree in Sosomolahun to listen.

"Crocodile had reached the top of the rock.

"Lizard sang again, louder than ever.

" *'Eagle, eagle, please come!*
A crocodile has seen your child.
Linkpin, a linkpin, lakpan.'

"This time Eagle understood. She flew straight home. The crocodile had just reached Eagle's nest.

" 'Mother, mother!' screamed the baby eagle.

"Eagle grabbed the crocodile with the talons on

her feet and flew up in the air. Then she opened her talons.

"Crocodile landed in the river. If he had landed on the ground, he would have been killed. The water saved his life. That's why the crocodile always lives in water now."

At the end of the folktale, my mother had written: "This reminds me of us."

"This reminds my mother of us, Maud," I said. "She's the eagle, you see. And I'm the baby eagle. And Liz, Liz is the lizard. Liz, lizard! Even the name is the same! But who's the crocodile?"

Maud whined.

I folded the folktale back up and put it in the envelope. I would tell Matilda the folktale. Maybe I would tell Liz, too. It was *my* folktale, and I could do whatever I wanted with it. I got up and put the envelope in my pocket. Then I opened the bedroom door.

My father and Liz were standing next to the computer, but they weren't looking at it. My father was holding Liz very tight and kissing her. Their faces were all kind of mashed together, not like people kissing on TV. They didn't even see me.

I closed the bedroom door quickly and sat back down on the bed. I had never seen my father kiss anyone but my mother and my grandmother. He looked strange and so did Liz. I only saw Brad kiss my mother once, but their faces had that strange look, too. My stomach felt funny. I wanted my father and Liz to get married but I'd forgotten about the kissing.

I unfolded the folktale again.

"Amy!" It was my father's voice.

I opened the bedroom door.

"I'm leaving, Tulip," he said. He and Liz looked all right again, though her face was kind of red.

My father stooped down and kissed my cheek. Then he took Liz's hand and they walked toward the door. They kind of leaned together and I thought maybe they were going to start kissing again, but my father put his hand on the doorknob and smiled at us and went out. Liz stared at the door.

"I'm going down to Matilda's," I said.

Mrs. Matthews came to the door when I knocked. She said Matilda was in the basement, practicing.

When I got off the elevator, I listened but I couldn't hear anyone tap-dancing. Then I heard a voice coming from Al's office. The voice sounded like Tom Tyrell's.

". . . I'll never get this floor clean in time for the opening! What's that? Why, it's . . ."

"Pink Dragon!" shouted some voices.

In Al's office, Matilda and Al and John were all sitting down, watching Tom Tyrell. He was standing in the middle of the room, holding a mop.

"Amy!" said Tom Tyrell. "I was just rehearsing for my audition. Why don't you join the audience?"

"Audition for what?" I asked.

"For the Pink Dragon commercial!" said Matilda. "Mr. Tyrell would be this man who's cleaning a theater!"

"I like the Pink Dragon commercials," I said, sitting down next to Matilda. " 'Dragon Power—it slays dirt!' How do they get the people in the scene with the Pink Dragon?"

"First they film the dragon drawings and then they film the actors," said Tom Tyrell. "And finally they put the two films together. I have to pretend I'm seeing the dragon." He began to walk back and forth, pushing the mop. "Ground-in dirt!" he rumbled. "Grease! I'll never get this floor clean in time for the opening!"

He dropped his shoulders and looked very sad. Then he looked up. "What's that? Why, it's . . ."

"Pink Dragon!" Matilda and Al and John and I all screamed together.

"That was wonderful, Mr. Tyrell," said Matilda. "I'm sure you'll get the commercial."

"I hope so," said Tom Tyrell. "The residuals would be most helpful. But do you think I really look distressed when I'm pushing the mop? I should convey pain—even anguish!"

"Wellllllll," said Matilda, "maybe a little more pain. Don't you think so, Amy?"

"More pain," I agreed.

Al's phone rang and he went over to his desk and picked it up. "Yes, Mrs. Goldman," he said. "Uh-huh. How much water is there? Uh-huh. I think I can make it in about an hour." He hung up the phone and sat down.

Tom Tyrell did his part again, with more pain. Finally he said, "You've been a great help! How I love to see the faces of an audience—their joy, their tears! It inspires me! And now I must collect my clothes from the dryer."

"Let us know how the audition turns out, Mr. Tyrell," said Al, switching on the TV.

"Talent, real talent," said John when Tom Tyrell left. "He was the old storekeeper in the Softissima commercial, you know."

"And the stove repairman in the CleanAway ad," said Al, turning the dial.

There was the noise of a helicopter on the TV.

"Listen," I whispered to Matilda. "I've got lots to tell you."

Matilda got up. "I've seen this one, anyway."

We walked back down the hall.

"My mother sent me a letter!" I said. "There's a folktale in it just for me. And my father kissed Liz today, right in the apartment!"

Matilda's brown eyes grew very big. "Oh!" she said. "Did he really kiss her?"

"Yes. They were all kind of mashed together. It makes you feel weird to see your parents kissing someone that's not in the family."

"I know. My father and my stepmother used to kiss all the time. Before they got married, I mean. Once I found them kissing in the *closet* when I went to get my coat. It was so embarrassing."

"When I saw them kissing I went back in the bedroom and pretended I didn't see them."

"But you want them to get together, don't you?"

"Oh, sure. Sure. But real people kissing don't look anything like people on the soaps kissing."

"I know. I wonder why?"

"I don't know."

I took the folktale out of my pocket and smoothed it out. "This is the folktale," I said. "It's called 'The Eagle's Child.' "

"Oh, read it to me!"

"Okay. You'll be the first person to hear it. Let's sit down in the laundry room."

We sat on the bench people sit on while they're waiting for their clothes to get washed. " 'Once Eagle laid her egg in a nest of sticks on a big rock,' " I began.

Matilda liked the folktale a lot. It was almost time for dinner, so we went out and stood in front of the elevators. "This is the step we learned this week," said Matilda. "Ruby Keeler does it in *Footlight Parade.*"

She danced down the hall.

"It looks hard," I said.

"Well, it is, a little. It's left, right, left, right, one two, three, four, turn. See?"

"Slower."

So she did it slower, and just as the elevator came, I almost had it.

"Ruby Keeler wears a sailor hat in *Footlight Parade,*" said Matilda, shuffling her feet on the elevator floor.

"I saw a hat like that in the thrift shop on the corner. But it was seven dollars. I have to save my money just in case."

"Pink's reward," said Matilda. "Oh, Amy, I just know Pink's alive. Somewhere!"

I shook my head. I didn't want to think about Pink being alive. Because then I'd feel too bad if I found out he had been killed by the wild rats.

When I got back to the apartment, Liz was in the kitchen, making dinner. "Amy, do you think you could stay with Matilda on Saturday night?" she called out. "Carl and I would like to go to the special benefit concert for the zoo and we'll probably get back late."

They didn't even ask me to go to the special benefit concert for the zoo! There was going to be an elephant there and I would have liked to see it.

"I guess so," I said. I went into the bedroom and banged the door closed after me.

I opened Pink's cage and turned the little wheel. "Maybe, Pink, getting my father and Liz together wasn't such a good idea after all," I said.

Chapter Nine

◆

M atilda, do you know what?" I said. "My father's taking Liz to an Off-Off Broadway show this week and he didn't ask me! And he took Liz to Shakespeare in the Park and the free concert on the pier last week and he didn't ask me! And the week before he took her all the way up-town to the Cloisters, and he didn't ask me!"

We were sitting on the laundry room bench. I could see my laundry going round and round inside one of the machines.

"Well, you did all go roller-skating at the rink," said Matilda.

"That was weeks and weeks ago!" I said. "Now my father sees lots more of Liz than he does of *me!*"

"They're having a romance, you know. On the soaps, people who are having romances always want to be alone."

"But I practically never see my father anymore except when he comes to dinner!"

I stared at the clothes going round and round. When I had my great idea about getting my father and Liz together, it was so I could be with him more. But it wasn't working out the way I'd thought. He wanted to be with Liz more than he wanted to be with me! And they kept doing these embarrassing things. Once when I went into the kitchen to get another piece of Liz's pecan pie, they were kissing right in front of the refrigerator!

Al and Harry, the handyman, went past the laundry room door, pushing the new cleaning machine. The building management bought the machine after lots of people complained about the dirty floors at the tenants' meeting. They complained about the elevators and Howie sleeping, too, but nothing had happened about them.

"It's no fun when your father is having a romance," I said.

"When my father was having *his* romance, I practically never saw him at all," said Matilda. "Of course I see him now he's married. And you will, too. But it'll be different because then there'll be the baby."

I turned to look at her. "The what?"

"The baby," said Matilda. "When it comes they don't pay much attention to you. They play with the baby all the time. I think babies are awfully uninteresting."

"A baby!" I said. I could feel myself turning all cold even though it was warm in the basement. A baby! "Would Liz have a *baby?*" I asked.

"Well, probably," said Matilda. "She'll have to have one soon, you know, or she'll be too old. How old is Liz?"

"Thirty-three," I said. "A baby!" And then this picture came into my mind of my father and Liz in the new apartment. He was painting and she was working at her computer. And I was in the extra room watching the used color TV. Only it wasn't the extra room anymore. It was the baby's room.

The baby yelled and Liz rushed over to it. So did my father. "Hey!" I said. "Hey, what about me?" But nobody noticed me.

The clothes had stopped going round and round in the dryer, so I opened the door and put them in the basket. But I couldn't seem to move fast. It was like I was in a dream. A baby!

While we were waiting for the elevator, Matilda

said: "Amy, you've dumped all the T-shirts on the floor!"

"Oh," I said, looking down.

"Don't stand there, help me pick them up," said Matilda.

We picked the T-shirts up but there wasn't time to fold them before the elevator came. So we lumped them all together in the basket.

"Are you sick?" asked Matilda. "You look weird."

I looked at her. "Maybe getting my father and Liz together wasn't such a great idea after all," I said. "I didn't think about a baby."

"It's too late *now*. They're having a romance."

When we reached Matilda's floor, she said, "Why don't you ask your father to take you somewhere we can all go together? Like, you know, a picnic."

I just stared at her. "I'll call you," Matilda's voice said through the door as it closed.

I rode up to the eighth floor. Too late now, I thought as I went down the hall. Too late now. But maybe it wasn't too late! Maybe I could sort of— turn off the romance! But how? Then I heard the phone ringing. It sounded like it was coming from 8-J. Liz wasn't there today. I ran down the hall.

"Hello," I said, all out of breath.

"Hello," said a woman's voice. "Is this Amy?"

"Yes."

"It's Janine, Amy. How's the Fumalee rain poncho?"

"Oh! Oh, it's . . . fine!"

"It's waterproof, you know. I'm calling because I've had this great idea!"

"Oh," I said. I didn't want to hear about anybody else's great ideas. Great ideas weren't so great sometimes. Why had I ever tried to get my father and Liz together? A baby!

"Do you know it's your father's thirty-fifth birthday next Sunday?"

"Is it?" I'd forgotten.

"The thirty-fifth birthday is a kind of milestone, if you know what I mean. So I thought I'd give him a surprise party in my apartment. Some of his friends down here will hide and sort of pop out when he comes in!" Janine laughed, a low sound like she was gargling. "It'll be fun. And I'd like you to come, of course. I'm hoping we can see lots more of each other, Amy. In fact, I'm weaving something just for you right now."

Suddenly I felt sick to my stomach. Janine is the crocodile, I thought.

"Are you there, Amy?"

"Yes," I said. "We're, we're giving a party for my father in the park on Sunday. It's a picnic party. Yes! We've been planning for weeks and weeks! We're going to have, um, fried chicken and, um, potato salad. It's just for his *family*."

"Family? Who's that?"

"Well me, of course. And his, um, brother. And his niece, his niece, my cousin Matilda!"

"I didn't know he had a brother and a niece in the city."

"They live in New Jersey. But they're coming in for the picnic." I should add some more people, I thought. "And his, um, aunt is coming, too. Yes, Aunt Maud. From Pennsylvania."

"I see." Janine's voice wasn't warm anymore. "On Saturday I have to go out of town. So Sunday was the only day. Well, it's too bad. I don't think your father is really the picnic type, you know." She hung up.

I dialed my father's number. What if Janine gets there first? She's right in the building. Please, please make him answer.

"Hello."

"It's me. Daddy, can you take Liz and me on a picnic Sunday? Because it's your birthday."

"Yeah, I know," said my father. "The big thirty-five. It's creeping up."

"What?"

"Age. Let me check my calendar about Sunday."

That was a joke. He didn't have a calendar.

"Yes, I see Sunday is free—all day," said my father. "Where will this picnic be?"

"Um, um," I said, thinking fast. Somewhere far away so it would take the whole day. Then nobody would be home if Janine called. "The Bronx Botanical Garden," I said. I had been there once, when I was little. It was a long way on the subway, I remembered.

"Done!" said my father.

"Can Matilda go, too?" I asked. "And Maud?" Maud heard her name and put her paw on my leg.

"I won't go without Maud and Matilda," said my father. "Especially Maud."

After I hung up, I looked in the refrigerator for my lunch. It was there, with the sign that said Amy's Lunch. This time it was a chicken sandwich with lettuce and mayonnaise, and three tollhouse cookies. I sat at the table, reading my book. I finished the really good book a long time ago. I hated to see it end. It was like when my best friend moved to Scottsdale, Arizona. This book was by the same person who wrote the really good book but it wasn't as good. It was good, just not really, really good.

When I was finished with lunch I sat down in one of the living room chairs with the book. The pigeon was on the windowsill. Why didn't you ever see any baby pigeons? They must hide them. It was too bad human babies couldn't be like pigeon babies. If my father didn't get married to Liz and have a baby, he would marry Janine and have one. Except with Janine, he'd probably have more. Because she was young. And the apartment would be full of babies and the giant looms. There wouldn't be any room for me at all.

The phone rang. It was Matilda. "Are you all right?" she asked. "You looked really strange in the laundry room."

"Sort of," I said. "Can you go on a picnic with me and my father and Liz on Sunday?"

"A picnic! Oh, great!"

"Meet me and Maud in the lobby and we'll walk around the block," I said. "I've got something to tell you."

I put on Maud's leash. When I got to the lobby, Howie was walking up and down.

"Hi, Howie."

Howie nodded at me but he didn't stop walking. The elevator door opened and Matilda got out.

"Hi, Howie."

Howie nodded again but he still didn't stop walking.

"Howie," said Matilda when he came close to us, "what are you doing?"

"If I keep moving, I won't fall asleep," said Howie.

We walked with him. We had to so we could talk to him.

"Won't you get tired?" I asked as we marched by one of the metal sofas chained to the wall.

"I heard what people said at the tenants' meeting," said Howie. "People complained because I fall asleep all the time. Some of them said it's because I'm too old. Do you know how old I am?"

We shook our heads.

"Seventy-two! But I don't fall asleep because I'm seventy-two. No! I've always fallen asleep when I sit down. I used to fall asleep in P.S. 119."

Howie stopped so quickly we almost bumped into him. "The tenants want to fire me, don't they?" he asked.

"No!" said Matilda. "Well," she added, "maybe a couple of people do. But most of the tenants like you."

"Do they?"

We nodded.

Howie walked to the front door and stood looking out. "Fifty years ago I came here," he said. "It was a luxury building then." He pointed to the wall. "They had a statue right there! And the lobby was wallpapered!"

I remembered what Liz had said. "Howie, maybe you could ask a doctor for some medicine to keep you awake. Liz heard about a medicine like that."

"Did she?" asked Howie.

"Then you wouldn't have to keep walking," said Matilda.

Yap! Yap! Yap! Maud had heard the word *walk* and was jumping all around.

Matilda and I went out the door with Maud.

"Listen," I said to Matilda. "When I got back, Janine was on the phone. She wanted to give a surprise party for my father's thirty-fifth birthday next Sunday. So I told her we already were having a birthday picnic for him on Sunday!"

"Did you?" asked Matilda.

"Yes!"

"I never could have thought of that so fast," said Matilda.

"And he says he'll come! So it's all fixed."

"Do you suppose she'll find out that you just made up the birthday picnic right then?"

"I hope not. Janine said she was weaving something special for me!"

"How horrible!"

"I'd just die if I had to wear those awful woven things. You see, Matilda, Liz is just lots better than Janine, even with a baby. Besides, Janine's younger than Liz. She'd probably have more babies!"

Matilda nodded. "Definitely!"

We giggled.

Before I went back upstairs I looked in Liz's mailbox. There was lots of mail for Liz and two blue envelopes with Wambian stamps—one for me and another one for Liz!

As soon as I got to the apartment, I opened my letter and read it to Maud the dog. My mother got my letter, she wrote. She was very sorry about Pink. She paid a diviner in the village to find out what I should do about Pink. A diviner is someone who tells people what to do about their problems. This diviner threw a handful of little shells on the ground. Then he looked at the way the shells were lying on the ground.

"The diviner said, 'Wait,' " my mother wrote.

"Wait?" I said to Maud the dog. "Wait?" It didn't seem like much of a message to come all the way from Africa.

My mother said she had some good folktales already. She said she had bought me an animal mask with a jaw that moved up and down. She said she loved me and thought about me every day.

When Liz got back, I told her about the picnic.

"His thirty-fifth birthday," said Liz, with this big smile. "I'll make a cake!"

"Can we have fried chicken and potato salad?" I asked.

"It sounds delicious," said Liz. "We'll carry it in this picnic basket I have." She opened my mother's letter.

Liz smiled a lot now that she and my father were having a romance, and her eyes had this sparkly look, like Mrs. Goldman's ring.

"Do you ever think about having a baby?" I asked.

"What?" Liz looked up from her letter.

"A baby."

"I think about it sometimes," said Liz, putting

said. I went into the bedroom and put on the hat. Liz bought it for me at the thrift shop so that I could save my money for Pink's reward.

When my father came, he had a bottle of wine. "And a corkscrew," he said. "Never forget the corkscrew on a picnic. You look like someone in that hat, Tulip."

"Who?"

"A movie star, maybe."

"When we're outside," I said, "I'll give you a clue!"

When we went through the lobby, Howie pushed open the front door.

"I haven't seen Howie sleeping the last few days," said Liz.

As soon as we were outside the building, I said, "Here it is, Daddy, the clue!"

I danced the new step Matilda had been showing me.

"That's pretty good!" said my father. "Okay, you're a dancer. Donna McKechnie?"

I shook my head.

"I know—the cute one in those 1930s movies on TV—Ruby, Ruby Keeler—right?"

I nodded, happy. This was going to be a great picnic! We walked to the subway stop. The Bronx is part of New York City, too, but you have to take the subway a long way to get there. We all sat in a row on the subway, except Maud, who was in her dog carrier on the floor. There were lots of people on the subway. They all looked nice today. Some of them smiled at Maud in her dog carrier.

First the subway ran underground, the way it usually does. But then it came out of the ground and ran along on top. All around us were these funny old buildings without any grass between them. I didn't remember any of this.

"This doesn't look like a place for a garden," I said to Matilda, who was sitting next to me at the end of the row.

"You'll see," she said. She leaned her head toward me. "Liz looks so beautiful today," she whispered in my ear.

I looked at Liz. She was wearing a pink T-shirt, jeans, and a necklace with pink beads. Her black hair was all shiny in the sun coming through the windows. She was laughing at something my father was saying to her. My father was sitting very close to Liz and he had his arm around her arm.

We were so busy watching them that we didn't notice when we got to the Bronx Botanical Garden stop. Suddenly everybody was getting up.

"Here it is," said Liz.

Yap! Yap! Yap! Maud was barking inside her dog carrier. Outside the station, Liz opened the carrier and put her on the leash. Maud danced around. She was glad to get out.

We walked down this long street beside a high wall. You could see trees behind the wall. Finally we came to a big gate. Through it I could see trees and bushes and flowers.

"It *is* the garden," I said.

As soon as we got inside the gate, we saw this big house with all these flowers in front of it. I'd never seen so many flowers. We walked up and down rows and rows of them.

Liz stood at the end of a row of pink geraniums and clapped her hands together. "They're so beautiful!" she said.

"You're like a child sometimes," said my father, smiling and putting his hand on her arm.

Matilda and I looked at each other. "I hope they don't start kissing," I whispered.

After we looked at the flowers, we went to this big grassy lawn. Liz spread out the tablecloth under a tree. She took plates and forks and paper cups out of the picnic basket. Then she put out dishes of grapes and cheese and crackers.

My father put the corkscrew in the top of the little bottle of wine. Pop! The cork came out of the bottle. My father poured some wine into two paper cups. Liz poured some juice into two more paper cups.

"I love picnics," said Matilda.

Liz raised her paper cup in the air and touched my father's cup. "To picnics."

"To love," said my father, staring at Liz.

Matilda poked me. I was sure they were going to start kissing but Liz opened the hamper again. We ate all the food and drank most of the juice and wine. Then Liz took a tin box out of the picnic basket. She took off the lid, and inside was the little cake. On the top it said: "Thirty-Five."

My father gave Liz a kiss right on the mouth. Matilda and I looked at each other. I felt embarrassed, but I felt happy, too. My father and Liz would get married and have room for me!

Liz cut the cake and everyone had a piece, even Maud. Afterward we all sat around yawning.

"Why does eating food outside in the afternoon make you sleepy?" asked Liz.

"It's a chemical in the brain," said my father. "It's activated only by picnic food in the afternoon. Let's all take a nap."

We all lay down on the tablecloth in a row and looked up at the tree overhead.

"I'm going to do a painting of these tree branches against the sky," said my father. "I'll call it *Picnic*. And nobody will know why."

"Except us," I said.

"Except us," he said.

"This is a very special birthday," said my father. "I'll always remember it." He reached out for Liz's hand and then for mine. "Maybe it's worth turning thirty-five for a birthday like this."

I could see Liz smiling at him. She looked really beautiful.

When we got up, my father poured the rest of the wine into Liz's cup and his cup.

"I have some news," said Liz. She looked at all of us and smiled. "I met with my editor last week and I was telling her about Carl's work. She was quite interested! It seems they've acquired this wonderful picture book manuscript about trees but they can't find the right artist to do it. So I showed her the painting Carl gave me. And now she wants to look at slides of your paintings, Carl!"

"A picture book?" My father was frowning.

"Publishers are doing gorgeous picture books now—full color. And it could be a good career move for you at this time. People would notice your work." Liz touched my father's arm with her hand. "The money wouldn't be bad either—this is a major publisher."

"Wait a minute," said my father. "I don't do illustrations. I'm a *painter.*"

"Of course you are, Carl, a great painter. But you can do both. Look at Wanda Bottemly."

"Wanda Bottemly does trash!" said my father in a loud voice. He had the hard, shiny look in his eyes.

Some people who were having a picnic nearby looked up.

Matilda and I moved closer together. "They're

fighting," whispered Matilda. She looked scared. I felt scared, too. "Let's take Maud for a walk," I said. When I stood up, it was like when you shake a kaleidoscope and the whole scene slides into something else. The park looked all different. I started walking carefully, so I wouldn't fall down in this funny-looking world. How could my father be so happy one minute and so mad the next? I took Matilda's hand.

"Don't you understand anything?" My father was shouting as we walked away. "I went that route. I was an advertising illustrator—a very well paid one. Now I'm just a poor painter!"

"But, Carl, I was just trying to help!"

Hand in hand, Matilda and I walked Maud around the grassy field. I tried not to think about my father and Liz. We saw lots of squirrels and crows. And next to a garbage can we saw two gray animals with long skinny tails. They were eating something that had fallen out of the garbage can. I recognized them this time.

"Rats," I whispered.

One of the rats looked at me, a mean look. It had beady eyes, like the one I saw before. If poor Pink met a rat like that, he would be very scared. Pink! Where was Pink? Pink never shouted, never got that hard, shiny look in his eyes. I looked across the field. I could see my father and Liz. They weren't fighting anymore. My father was sitting with his arms folded, looking at the ground. Liz was putting stuff back in the picnic basket. She looked up and saw us. She waved to us to come back.

"We're leaving," said Liz when we got there.

My father and Liz didn't talk on the way back to the subway stop. Matilda and I didn't talk, either. When the subway came, it was crowded. The people all looked funny, not nice like they had before. We had to sit in different seats. Matilda was in the seat across from me. My thoughts went around and around, like the laundry in the dryer. My father and Liz fought. My mother and father fought. My father and mother got a divorce. My father and Liz wouldn't get married. A baby. Janine. No room.

I closed my eyes. The person next to me got off and Matilda sat next to me.

"I feel dizzy," I whispered.

"It's nerves," said Matilda. "Think about something nice." She held my hand.

"What?"

"Tap dancing."

So I thought about Ruby Keeler wearing her sailor hat and dancing. I felt better.

Just before we got to Liz's stop, the lady on the other side of me got off. My father sat down and gave my shoulders a squeeze.

"I'm going to my apartment," he said. "I'm sorry. I'll call you, okay? Next week we'll go somewhere, just the two of us."

"Okay." I didn't look at him. He had ruined our picnic. He had ruined my great idea.

The train was pulling into Liz's stop. My father took the dog carrier off the train and set it down on the platform. Then he got back on the train. From the corner of my eye, I could see him waving to me as the train pulled out. I pretended I didn't see him.

Liz was taking Maud out of the carrier. "Can you walk Maud, Amy? And, Matilda, maybe you can take the carrier. It doesn't weigh much when it's empty. I'll take the basket."

When we got to the door of the apartment building, Liz stopped and looked at us. "I'm sorry," she said. "Sorry that . . . well, I'm just sorry."

"It was a nice picnic most of the time, Ms. Farrelly," said Matilda.

Howie was wide awake when we went in. He leaped up and pressed the elevator button.

Matilda went up to the eighth floor with us so she could take the dog carrier to Liz's apartment. Inside the apartment, Liz put the picnic basket in the kitchen. "I think I'll lie down in the bedroom for a while, Amy," she said. "I'm—tired." She looked tired. There were lines on both sides of her mouth. I hadn't seen them before.

She went into the bedroom and closed the door. We heard a small sound behind the door.

"She's crying," said Matilda.

"I know. I hate it when grown-ups cry."

Matilda nodded. "I'd better go." She went out, closing the door softly behind her.

When grown-ups cry, it makes me afraid. I think grown-ups should always be brave. My mother hardly ever cries. My mother is brave. Liz is a scaredy-cat.

I couldn't look at TV because it was in the bedroom with Liz. So I got the book Matilda loaned me and tried to read it. But I couldn't. Why, I thought, did my father get so mad? It was just the way he was with my mother. But Liz wasn't like my mother. She didn't get mad back. My father was mad all by himself. I didn't like my father today.

He's the crocodile, I thought. He is.

I wished Pink were there! Pink was so warm, so cuddly. Pink never got mad or cried.

I got up and sat on the low table in front of the window, the one where Maud liked to sit and look out, even though all she could see were roofs. Maud was sitting there, looking out. I put my arm around her.

"Grown-ups are very hard to understand, Maud," I said.

Maud whined as if she agreed with me.

Chapter Eleven

———◆———

I put a little more orange in the pigeon's eye.

"You know," said Liz, "that's good. Really good." She was standing next to the table, looking at my drawing. I did it with a set of special colored pencils my father bought me. In back of the pigeon were rooftops, just like the rooftops outside Liz's window.

I leaned the drawing against the bowl on the

table and got up. I stood next to Liz. "Do you think the perspective is okay?" I asked.

"It's fine. You have an eye," said Liz. "Guess it runs in the family."

The drawing of the pigeon was a late birthday present for my father. After the picnic my father didn't call me or Liz. So I called him Wednesday when Liz went out.

"I'm making a late birthday present for you," I said. "It's a drawing."

"I'm clearing a space for it right now," he said. "When will it be ready?"

"On the weekend."

"Come down Sunday, Tulip. I'll pay for the taxi."

"Okay. Are you going to call Liz?"

"I don't think so, Tulip."

"Liz looks sad."

"Sorry." But he didn't sound sorry. "See you Sunday," he said.

That was today. I put the drawing carefully in this folder Liz loaned me and tied it with string. Then I sat down in a chair and picked up the comics in one of Liz's newspapers. I wasn't going to my father's until after lunch.

Liz was reading the *New York Times*. She put the paper down and looked at me. "Amy, when you see your father today, would you tell him something for me?"

"Okay."

"Tell him . . . tell him that I have the highest respect for his artistic achievements and commitment to his ideals. . . ."

There was more like that, with lots of long words. I looked out the window. The pigeon was there again. It looked at me.

Finally Liz stopped. I picked up the comics again.

"Amy. Don't tell your father that. Tell him I realize I was insensitive in trying to assess his potentialities and that . . ."

She went on and on. I looked out the window. The pigeon was walking up and down the ledge outside the window.

Liz picked up the paper, so I started reading the comics.

"Amy! Don't tell your father that, tell him that I was only trying to help him to utilize his creative abilities in the maximum. . . ."

The pigeon had flown away. It's nice to be able to fly.

When Liz went back to the paper, I got up and went into the bedroom before she could start talking again. I closed the bedroom door and turned on the TV. Someone wearing a long dress was singing a hymn. I turned to another program. Some men were sitting in chairs, talking. I tried to listen to what the men were saying but these thoughts kept sneaking in. I couldn't stop them.

Liz and my father wouldn't get married. My father wouldn't sell his paintings. My mother would be mad because he wouldn't give her any money. My father wouldn't have any room for me. I wouldn't see Matilda. And Pink was gone forever. I felt like I was this little feather, a little pigeon feather, that was being blown around by the wind. On the TV, the men in chairs went on talking. I switched it off.

"Amy! Lunch!"

After lunch Liz and I took Maud out for a walk. Howie jumped up out of his chair and ran over to the door to open it. "You seem very alert lately, Howie," said Liz.

"The doctor told me I have a medical condition," he said. "Makes me fall asleep when I sit down. It has nothing to do with age! So he gave me a prescription that keeps me awake."

"Really!" said Liz. She smiled at Howie.

It was just starting to rain but not very hard when we went out. A big gray car stopped in front of the apartment house and a man got out. He went around to the other side of the big car and opened the door. Mrs. Goldman got out. As soon as he saw her, Howie grabbed an umbrella and rushed out. The man kissed Mrs. Goldman and got back in the car. Howie held the umbrella over Mrs. Goldman's head before she got under the torn awning.

"I've just had lunch with my son Howard, Elizabeth," said Mrs. Goldman. "At the Peony!"

"The new in place, Helene!"

"Definitely! We saw Gloria *and* Pat. Thank you, Howie."

Howie winked at me behind Mrs. Goldman's back.

"Just think, it's almost August," said Liz as we walked toward the park. "In another month your mother will be coming home. It'll be strange, Amy, not having you here! I've gotten used to it."

"Won't you be glad to get your bed back?"

Liz smiled. "Yes. But I'll miss you, too. Why don't you come back next summer for a month?"

"I'd like to!" I could see Matilda for a month next summer!

By the time we got home, it was time to go to my father's. Liz went downstairs with me.

Howie was standing at the door, looking out at the rain. "Cab?" he asked. As soon as Liz nodded, he almost ran out the door to the street and started waving his arm.

We stood under the torn awning, waiting. "Amy," said Liz. "Forget all those things I told you to tell your father."

"Okay."

"Just tell him one thing. That I think he's a great artist."

"Okay. I'll tell him."

A taxi stopped in front of the apartment house. Liz hugged me.

My father met me outside his building. "This is for you," I said, giving him the folder.

My father's apartment was even more crowded than the last time I'd been there. Because now there was this great big painting of a green tree right in the middle. The funny thing about this painting was that it was in three pieces but the pieces went together, like a screen.

"A triptych," said my father. "That means three parts."

"The tree is green."

"Back to the basics. I'm into green trees now."

I walked right up to the triptych. The two sides of it came out around me. "It's like I've climbed into a tree, a real tree."

"My favorite critic." My father kissed the top of my head and opened the folder. He took out the drawing and put it on the table, against a milk carton. He stood back and looked at it.

I held my breath. My father doesn't like lots of art. But when he turned around, he was smiling a big smile.

"This is strong, Amy." He hugged me. "Thank you. We have two artists in the family now."

He walked along the wall. "Here! A bit of rubber cement and . . ."

"It looks nice there," I said.

"We needed a little animal life."

There was a new cloth folded up on the table. "Janine," I said, picking up a corner of the cloth."

"Right. Sit down." He waved to the sofa.

I moved a pile of magazines and sat down. My father sat in a folding chair.

"How's Cousin Matilda? And Aunt Maud?"

He knew. I looked at him, scared. Was he going to be mad at me?

But he was smiling and he reached out and took my hand. "You don't like Janine," he said.

"I like Liz better, *lots* better."

"I'm glad you and the Godmother are getting along."

"She gave me a message for you."

"Oh?"

"She said: 'Tell him I think he's a great artist.' "

My father got up. He walked around the room. "Not too many people think I'm a great artist," he said.

He kept walking but there were all these things in the room so he had to keep walking around them. I watched him walk.

"Are you and Liz—are you going to get married someday?"

"No!" My father looked angry. "Why should I get married? I didn't make much of a success of it the first time."

I swallowed. There was this big lump in my throat. I wanted to say that if he got married to Liz she would clean up the apartment so he could walk around. And I wanted to say that he could have a real table to eat off, one that wasn't covered with paints. And I wanted to say that Liz would help sell his paintings. And I wanted to say that they could live in a big apartment with room for me. And I wanted to say that then I could see Matilda all summer and maybe other times, too.

But I couldn't say any of that. The words just wouldn't come out around the lump. So I said, "You could be—happy."

"Happy!" said my father with a terrible look on his face. "Happy!"

Tears started coming out of my eyes. I couldn't stop them. But my father wasn't looking at me. He was walking faster and faster. He bumped into his triptych.

"Most people aren't happy," said my father in this loud voice. "Am I supposed to be any different?"

He *was* the crocodile! He was the one who was doing something bad to me! I jumped up. But there wasn't anywhere to go in my father's apartment. I opened the front door.

"Tulip!"

I was running down the hall.

"Tulip! Tulip!" My father was running faster

than I was. He ran by me and stooped down, holding his arms out.

I ran into his arms. "You're the crocodile!" I cried. "You're the crocodile!"

"Tulip, Tulip. My poor Tulip. Let's go back to the apartment. We'll sit down and talk, talk nicely."

But when we got back I couldn't talk, only cry into my father's lap. "Poor Tulip," he said, smoothing my hair. "You've had a hard time. What do you mean, I'm the crocodile?"

"I won't tell you."

"Okay. Listen. A man in my position, my financial position, can't afford to get married. Besides, I want to be free, free to fail—or succeed—my own way. Do you see?"

I shook my head. "Are you going to marry Janine?"

"I'm not going to marry anybody," said my father. "Besides, Janine is in love with a designer who teaches at Pratt."

"Really?"

"I swear it. Tell me about the crocodile."

"No."

My father patted my shoulder. "There's a folk singer at the pier today. Let's go over there."

When we came back, we had take-out Chinese food on the floor on Janine's cloth. Then we looked at a program on the color TV until it was time to go home. "I'll get you a cab," said my father. He opened his wallet and looked inside. He looked mad. But then he smiled. "I'll take you home on the subway."

We had to walk a long way to the subway.

"Tell me about the crocodile," said my father as we walked down the street. He was holding my hand.

"Once there was an eagle who laid her egg on a big rock," I began.

"It's your mother's folktale," he said when I was finished.

"She said it reminded her of us."

We went down in the subway and the train came in with a roar. When we came up the stairs at Liz's stop, my father pointed to the sky. There was a big white moon shining through the clouds, even though it was still light.

"I'm not the crocodile," said my father. "Did you know father eagles take care of their children, just like mother eagles do?"

"Do they?" I asked.

"Check it out. Maybe I haven't done such a good job of taking care of you, but I'll always be in your corner, okay? I love you. I'm an eagle, too."

"Then who's the crocodile?" I asked.

"Ah!" said my father. "That's always the question."

He squeezed my hand and we walked down the

street to Liz's building. I felt very happy. My father loved me. And so did my mother. They were both eagles and they would always help me.

When we were about halfway down the street, I saw somebody standing in front of the building, somebody short. The somebody waved at us and then started running toward us.

It was Matilda!

"Amy!" she cried. "He's found! Pink is found!"

"Pink! Is he all right?"

"He's—fine," said Matilda, out of breath. "Liz called your father's apartment but you'd left. Hello, Mr. Schultz."

"Hello, Matilda. Where was Pink found?"

"That's the best part!" said Matilda, taking a deep breath. "Pink was in Tom Tyrell's garden! Tom Tyrell is in Ms. Farrelly's apartment. And so is Mrs. Goldman!"

I remembered something. "The diviner! He said to wait. And he was right!" So then I had to tell them about the diviner.

We were in front of the apartment house. I held on to my father's hand with both of mine. "Come upstairs with me to see Pink, please, please!" I said.

He smiled. "All right."

Howie threw open the door. The elevator was already on the first floor. He dashed over to it and pushed the button inside. "Eighth floor express!" he said. "I'm glad your rat is found, Amy."

"Thanks!" I said.

Matilda and I ran down the hall to Liz's apartment with my father behind us. Inside, Liz and Tom Tyrell and Mrs. Goldman were all sitting on the living room sofa, drinking something out of tiny glasses. Pink's cage was on the coffee table and inside it was . . .

"Pink!" I yelled.

I ran to the coffee table and put my fingers on the cage right next to Pink's nose. He sniffed my fingers, his whiskers moving very fast.

"It's me, Pink, Amy!"

"Carl!" said Liz. I could hear her introducing my father to Mrs. Goldman and Tom Tyrell.

Pink put his little pink paws up on the wall of the cage and looked right at me. His whiskers moved faster than ever.

"He remembers me!" I said.

Yap! Yap! Yap!

It was Maud the dog barking, but she sounded very far away.

"Maud's in the bedroom," said Liz. "I thought Pink should get used to being here before he met Maud again. Carl, why don't you have a glass of sherry with us? We're celebrating Pink's return."

I turned around. "Stay!" I said, grabbing his hand.

"Okay," he said.

Liz poured some stuff from a bottle into another little glass. Then she got some root beer for Matilda and me.

"How did you find Pink, Mr. Tyrell?" I asked.

"This evening, Helene and I were enjoying a light supper on my terrace," rumbled Tom Tyrell, nodding at Mrs. Goldman. "The rain had stopped. We noticed that the flowers were sparse in some areas."

Mrs. Goldman jumped in. " 'Thomas,' I said, 'something is eating those flowers—definitely!' " Mrs. Goldman was wearing a shiny dress. Earrings sparkled underneath her white hair.

Tom Tyrell raised his hands in the air. " 'Eating the flowers?' I asked. 'What creature would eat my flowers?' "

"And I said, 'Many animals eat plants, Thomas. Deer. Cows. Even rats.' " Mrs. Goldman nodded her head.

Tom Tyrell opened his eyes very wide. "We looked at each other. Two minds with but a single thought! As one person, we exclaimed: 'Amy's white rat!' "

"Go on!" I cried.

Holding a finger to his lips, Tom Tyrell looked at us. "I knew we had to be careful. A rat is a nervous beast—full of fears. I called Elizabeth. She came up with the cage. We put in a lovely chunk of aged Liederkranz I had been saving for a special occasion. Then we put the cage in the petunia bed."

"Because some of the petunias were missing," said Mrs. Goldman.

"And then we all had a glass of iced tea," put in Liz, smiling.

"And when we checked on the cage, we found Pink inside, eating the cheese!" said Tom Tyrell. "He didn't even try to leave!"

"It's his home," I said. I kissed Pink's nose through the cage.

"Oh, Amy," said Liz.

"Pink has been in Mr. Tyrell's garden all along!" cried Matilda. "He didn't go downstairs, he went upstairs!"

"He picked the best place in the building to go!" I said. "He's smart!"

"Definitely!" said Mrs. Goldman, looking at Tom Tyrell. He looked back and squeezed her hand.

All the tiny glasses were empty and so were our glasses. Liz filled them all again.

Tom Tyrell stood up. "And now, I have two announcements to make. First, I'm going to be the janitor in the Pink Dragon commercials!" When we finished cheering, he held up his glass and looked at Mrs. Goldman. "Second, next Sunday evening Helene and I will be married on the terrace. An informal ceremony. We hope you will all join us."

Matilda and I looked at each other, our mouths open. Mr. Tyrell and Mrs. Goldman are so old, I thought. Everybody started talking at once. Then Liz asked, "Where will you live?"

"In penthouse B," said Mrs. Goldman. "Imagine me giving up a rent-controlled apartment at my age—seventy-four!"

"I'm seventy-six!" said Tom Tyrell. "Naturally, I have fears about taking such a step! But Helene has such strength! An artist needs a strong partner."

I whispered to Matilda, "All this time, Tom Tyrell and Mrs. Goldman were having a romance and we didn't know anything about it!" And inside, I thought, You never know what grown-ups are going to do, never.

My father was saying something to Liz. She looked up at him, her face serious. Then she smiled. My father squeezed her hand.

"Look at your father and Liz," whispered Matilda. "Maybe . . ."

"Maybe," I said. "You never know what grown-ups are going to do. But no matter what, *we'll* always be friends."

Matilda smiled. "Always!" she said.

In his cage, Pink was looking all around. He was looking for me! I picked up the cage and touched his soft nose with one finger. "I'm right here, Pink."

Across the room, my father saw me and Pink, and smiled over Liz's shoulder. He raised his hand. "You see, Pink," I said. "I love you. So I'll always be on your side. And don't you forget it."

Barbara Ford was born in Saint Louis, grew up in a suburb of Pittsburgh, and returned to Saint Louis for college. She then lived and worked in New York City for a number of years, eventually becoming a full-time writer and moving to Mendham, New Jersey, where she now resides. Ms. Ford has written many nonfiction books for children, as well as magazine articles for adults; this is her first novel.

The folktale "The Eagle's Child" was actually collected in Liberia by the author's sister.